IN PURSUIT OF A GENTLEMAN

IN
PURSUIT OF A
Gentleman

FOREVER AFTER

ARLEM HAWKS

Cover design: Blue Water Books
Cover photo (model): Erica Shifflet

Arlem Hawks
www.arlemhawks.com

First printing: November 2019

To my parents, who fostered in me a love of tradition and always kept alive the magic of Christmas, no matter our circumstances.

"'I've run away from a little old woman,
A little old man,
A barn full of threshers,
A field full of mowers,
A cow and a pig,
And I can run away from you, I can!'
"Then the fox set out to run. Now foxes can run very fast, and so the
fox soon caught the gingerbread boy and began to eat him up.
"Presently the gingerbread boy said: 'O dear! I'm quarter gone!' And
then: 'Oh, I'm half gone!' And soon: 'I'm three-quarters gone!' And at
last: 'I'm all gone!' And never spoke again."

From "The Gingerbread Boy" in St. Nicholas Magazine,
Vol. II, May 1875

Chapter One

Market Foxley, Shropshire, England
November 1817

*A*ndrew Backus tugged up the collar of his greatcoat and shuffled past the shop as fast as the icy streets and his too-polished boots would allow him. Mrs. Thresher and her daughter had entered the milliner's shop down the street a few moments before without noticing him, and he wanted to keep it that way.

Minuscule snowflakes drifted lazily around him, just enough to speckle his face and clothing with wetness that stung in the chill air. If he hadn't needed a new neckerchief, he would not have ventured out into the threat of a storm. Or worse, the threat of encountering young ladies like Miss Thresher and their salivating mothers.

It wasn't as if he were really an heir worthy of their attention. They should have been chasing Steven.

Andrew glanced at the window just in time to see Mrs. Thresher snatch her daughter's hand and bolt towards the door. Dash it all, she'd seen him. He increased his speed, practically skating along the street. The tinkling bells from the milliner's door urged him faster, and he grabbed onto the side of the building to swing himself around the corner. This wretched snow! London didn't have nearly so much as Shropshire.

"Oh, Mr. Backus!" the matron's syrupy voice called behind him.

Andrew chuckled. If she thought she could catch him, she'd be terribly disappointed. But he had to find a place to hide if he didn't want to keep running all over town.

A little shop stood several paces down the road, a cheery glow through its windows lighting the dull afternoon. Andrew ran, slipping and sliding towards the sign that read "Hinwick's" above the establishment.

"Good day to you, Mr. Backus!" Mrs. Thresher's voice was muffled by the corner of the building she had not yet reached. He had only moments.

Puffs of his breath trailed behind him as he reached the shop. His feet skidded out from under him, and he grabbed the door handle, stomach leaping, before he hit the slushy street. Mrs. Thresher's cherry cloak whisked around the corner as he launched himself into the shop and slammed the door. Andrew pressed himself into the corner behind the entrance, out of sight of the windows.

"How did he not hear my greeting?" Mrs. Thresher's voice rang, getting louder. Andrew closed his eyes and burrowed deeper into the corner. "That man cannot keep running from marriage. And we will fix him, will we not, my dear?"

Fix him? Ha! Little chance of that.

A spicy scent tickled Andrew's nose. Small tables and chairs were scattered around the front of the shop, with a counter at the back where a middle-aged shopkeeper stood. Rustic paintings of wintery scenes hung on the walls. Baskets heaped high with round loaves and fist-sized rolls sat behind the counter. A bakery. He'd forgotten there was one in this section of town.

In the center of the room, a young woman sat with a cup of tea. She had a familiar look about her, though she wasn't one of the Market Foxley residents. Twenty years living with his aunt and uncle had made him well acquainted with the town's female offerings. The fine young lady's eyes flitted from him to the window.

Mrs. Thresher's voice blasted in, so deafening through the closed door she might as well have entered the shop. "Well, he did not come in here." Her voice carried through the glass panes of the window, sounding squished as if she pressed her face against the glass.

Andrew flattened himself against the corner so hard he was sure the doorframe put dents in his back.

"He must have gone round the corner. Hurry, Mary, or we shall lose him!" Her shouts faded up the street.

A sly smile crept over the lips of the young woman sipping tea. "Your pursuers have gone, sir."

Andrew heaved a sigh, letting his shoulders collapse. Thank the snowy heavens. He wiped his sleeve under the brim of his hat and pulled off his greatcoat, now too warm after his run.

"Would you like some refreshment after your exertion, sir?" the older woman behind the counter asked.

No harm in waiting to make sure the Threshers had gone. "Yes, thank you."

"That was quite the rush to get out of their grasp," the young lady said. He had seen that glint in her green eyes before. Her brilliant red hair fell out of a white bandeau in ringlets. The hair ornament matched the color of her morning gown and delicate fichu that covered her neck. He saw no coat. Had the shopkeeper stowed it for her?

"Yes, I cannot seem to go anywhere without a chase." Not like in London. He'd been nearly invisible in crowds of much wealthier and equally detached young men. "Might I sit with you, Miss…?"

"Todd." The young lady set her cup down and rose to give him a curtsy. "We met in Cheltenham some time ago."

Ah, that was it. "Of course. When I traveled there with my aunt and uncle for his health. We met at the assembly?" He vaguely remembered a sprightly red-haired dance partner from that holiday. But his aunt had not allowed him time to ask her for a second dance before whisking them all away from the party.

She smiled. "Yes, at Rooke's. Please, sit."

He hung his greatcoat across the back of the chair, droplets of melted snow raining onto the floor, and let his hat hang off the chair's corner. They both sat, and Miss Todd plucked up a biscuit resting beside her teacup. "How is your uncle's health?"

Andrew's gaze dropped to his gloves. He wished he could give a better answer. That would solve, at least temporarily, so many of his problems. "Much the same as it was two years ago."

"I am sorry to hear it."

Andrew waved it off. "What brings you to Market Foxley? We cannot boast healing waters or as good society as Cheltenham." Though he had been a long time in Town, he did not remember there being any Todds living near his aunt and uncle's country manor.

The shopkeeper bustled into the sitting area holding a tray set with a steaming cup of tea and a plate of long, slender biscuits like the one Miss Todd ate.

"Oh, I will only take the tea, thank you," Andrew said. He couldn't be there all day, though in the company of Miss Todd's fetching smile, he was tempted to delay.

Miss Todd snatched the plate from the tray, ignoring his refusal. "You must have Aunt Keppel's gingerbread. I insist. It is the very best gingerbread in the country."

Andrew nodded his thanks to the shopkeeper, who smiled at Miss Todd before returning to the kitchen. He picked up a biscuit and held it to his nose. This had been the sharp perfume he'd caught on entering the shop. Her aunt's gingerbread certainly smelled divine.

He paused and cocked his head. "Your aunt's?"

Miss Todd nodded through a bite of gingerbread. "Mr. Keppel is my mother's youngest brother."

And very below her station if he was a baker. Andrew's brows pulled together. The Todds were among the wealthier families of Cheltenham, if he remembered correctly from his visit. How had the uncle been reduced to a working-class businessman? Andrew bit into the gingerbread, the biscuit snapping pleasantly under his teeth. Cinnamon, ginger, and allspice flamed across his tongue, tempered to a satisfying heat by the dark, sweet notes of treacle. Her uncle made a fine gingerbread for being a former gentleman.

"He fell in love with my aunt and was disinherited," Miss Todd said, as though reading his thoughts. "His wife's father gave them the bakery on his death. Only my mother has continued a correspondence with him, though an infrequent one, and I am the single member of the family who deigns to visit." She pursed her lips. "And as my parents could not care where I am or what I am about, I like to spend Christmas in Market Foxley."

She said it so disinterestedly with a flip of her hand, and yet an edge crept into her voice. Something about the relation bothered her, either her greater family's ignoring the youngest uncle or the inattention of her parents. Perhaps both. It was no wonder he hadn't met her here before. He rarely stayed the winter with his aunt and uncle.

"Surely your parents are concerned with the whereabouts of such a lovely daughter." He hadn't meant it to sound so flirtatious. *Careful, Andrew. You'll have this one after you as well.*

But Miss Todd shook her head, not falling prey to the compliment. "I am the youngest of nine children. When they are not fussing over my sisters' babies, they are consumed with finding my brothers wives." She gave a wry grin as she dipped her nearly finished biscuit into her tea. "No matter what I do, they hardly give me any notice. I suppose that is why I feel so at home with my uncle, another forgotten youngest child."

So candid, for him being an unfamiliar acquaintance. A wistfulness had seeped into her tone, as though she had kept in this story for too long.

Andrew opened his mouth to respond, when a sliver of red through the window flashed across the corner of his vision. The Threshers! Miss Todd had distracted him from his aim. He bolted back for the corner behind the door, the only place out of sight of the windows. The chair he'd occupied came crashing down under the weight of his greatcoat, flipping his hat across the room and pinning the coat to the ground in an inelegant heap.

Miss Todd's eyes tracked across the length of the window, a droll lift at the corners of her pink lips as Mrs. Thresher's voice grew in volume. It seemed to stop before the door.

"Where can he have disappeared to? Exasperating man."

Andrew's heart leaped into his throat as the door opened and a blast of frigid air whistled through the tea room.

Isabella Todd averted her eyes and lifted her cup of tea, attempting not to snort into it as a generously trimmed bonnet poked into the bakery, blocking her view of the squashed Mr. Backus. The single bell above the door gave a cheery ring.

"Pardon my interruption, but have you seen Mr. Andrew Backus?" It was the younger woman who had passed by earlier. Miss Thresher. They'd met on a previous visit.

Isabella widened her eyes innocently. "Mr. Who?"

Miss Thresher huffed. She was near Isabella's twenty years, with brown hair and a thick pair of brows that starkly contrasted against her pale skin. What Mama wouldn't give for Isabella to look like that, with brown, unassuming hair. Never mind the permanent sneer.

"Backus. You have been away from Market Foxley too long, Miss Todd." The young woman put one foot through the door as though debating if she wished to enter. "Every young lady in twenty miles knows who Mr. Andrew Backus is."

Isabella set down her cup and took another finger of gingerbread. She would need to let out her clothes by the end of this holiday. "Then I shall endeavor to become better informed during my stay in Shropshire. He sounds like an intriguing man."

The young lady sniffed. "At three thousand pounds per annum, yes, I should say he is rather intriguing. After the will is rewritten, of course, but that is a certain thing." Her gaze fell to the floor, where Mr. Backus's coat and chair had fallen. "Is that not Mr. Backus's coat and hat?"

"Whose coat?" Isabella fought to keep the corners of her mouth from twitching. She attempted to smother the movement in a bite of gingerbread. The memory of Miss Thresher's pride had slipped her mind from her last visit.

The young woman's eyes narrowed. She scanned Isabella from head to toe, then took in the second cup across the table. She leaned in further to sweep the room with her gaze, lingering on the counter in the back, and looked ready to enter the shop for a more thorough investigation.

"You are letting in a monstrous chill," Isabella said.

That earned her a withering glare, which she met with another look of naïveté.

"Good day to you, Miss Thresher," Isabella turned back to her drink.

With a harrumph, the young woman backed out and shut the door behind her with a bang. The bell chortled after her, drowning out the mother and daughter's exclamations. Like a rabbit hiding from a hound, Mr. Backus didn't move an inch until the women's voices had retreated down the street once more.

"Are you so very scared of a pair of ladies?" Isabella teased when he pulled himself out of the corner. Whatever pomatum he'd put in his chestnut hair that morning had not done its job, as several strands had fallen forward nearly to his eyes. He brushed them back, but they would not return to join the rest of what had once been fashionably styled hair.

Mr. Backus retrieved his hat and returned the chair before taking his seat. "I wish they were the only ones. They are after my uncle's fortune and Birchill Manor, which are not even rightfully mine." He caught up the biscuit he'd dropped in his flight and chomped down in agitation.

"But they will be." Hadn't Miss Thresher said three thousand pounds? It was a respectable income, and though nothing to crow about among the London set, it would make him the most eligible bachelor in many country villages. No wonder all of Market Foxley had their sights set on Mr. Backus.

"They shouldn't come to me," he grumbled. "They are willed to my brother, but his prolonged illness has sent everyone speculating that I will be named the new heir at any moment." He shook his head.

Nearly an heir, then. And not under agreeable circumstances. An unentailed estate could easily change heirs before its owner's death. "Does your uncle plan to change his will?" It seemed a certain thing to Miss Thresher. Was his brother's illness so serious? She hoped not.

Mr. Backus leaned back in his chair. For a few moments, only the crackling of the fire in the hearth and the shuffling of Uncle and Aunt Keppel in the kitchen sounded through the room. The gentleman stared at his tea. He had a pleasant face, his firm jaw neatly shaved and eyes matching the shade of the spicy biscuits on the plate between them.

"If my aunt gets her wish, I will be the heir," he finally said.

Then perhaps there was more to it than simply the illness. Something tapped at the back of Isabella's mind. She couldn't brush it away. "But you hope she doesn't."

Mr. Backus gave his head a shake, returning the carefree grin that had once graced his visage. "No, I wish to continue as I have since finishing at university. I wish to return to London, enjoy my cards and my parties and my friends, and let others attend to the dreaded responsibility of running an estate. My aunt usually gets her own way, but I hope for once to thwart her." He downed the rest of his tea in a manner too hurried to be polite.

Isabella's pulse quickened as an odd idea took shape. "I hope you get your desires."

Mr. Backus rose and swung his greatcoat over his shoulders. "As do I. For now, I have promised my aunt to stay until January when Society begins its descent on London for the Season. So I must avoid the marriage hunters and hope the weeks pass quickly."

"Of course." Isabella stood, surveying her companion. Would he do? He had a trim form, with the perfect blend of fashion and nonchalance about his appearance. An inch or two more in height would render him perfect, as he was quite average in that aspect, but his amiable air made up for it.

He pressed his topper firmly onto his head and threw her a smile. "You must forgive me, I have said too much about my affairs."

Not too eager. "With eight siblings, it should not surprise you that I often have the opportunity to listen to others' woes. I do not mind listening. Especially when I can drink tea and eat gingerbread while doing it."

He laughed and pulled his gloves from his pocket along with a coin, which he set on the table. "Thank Mrs. Keppel for a fine refreshment. It was good to meet you again, Miss Todd." He bowed deeply, fingers on his hat.

"A pleasure, sir." Isabella returned his gesture with a curtsy.

As the door shut behind him, she ran her tongue over her lips, catching the lingering crumbs from her repast. Mama and Papa were in London with Isabella's sister for Christmas. If she could bring back a suitor, or even an engagement, surely they would pay her the notice they'd rarely bestowed. And three thousand pounds could not be ignored. Neither of her sisters had snared a husband worth that much.

Yes, he would do nicely for Mama and Papa.

Isabella sank into her chair, watching the snow lightly swirling past the window. She would have to proceed with caution. The moment Mr. Andrew Backus caught wind that she was in pursuit as much as any of his Market Foxley neighbors, her plan would be forfeit. She had less than two months until January, when the *ton* began trickling back into London, and with them her target. Less than two months to draw her parents' praise for once in her life.

She tapped the table, not allowing herself to linger on their lack of regard. Feeling sorry for herself had done nothing all these years. This plan could work, and if it didn't, at least she would add some fun to this dreary winter. Not every year did a young lady have the chance to spend Christmas in pursuit of a gentleman who had no desire to be caught. And that challenge in itself was altogether too tempting.

Chapter Two

Andrew met the physician in the corridor as the man came down the stairs with his medical bag. Though tempted to brush past after nodding a greeting, he stopped the doctor with a hand on his arm.

"Any news?"

The greying man sighed. "No changes to your older brother's situation."

Andrew had expected that. Steven hadn't left his room in weeks.

"Your uncle is in stable condition, but I fear for his health as the winter progresses. Any additional illness could prove difficult to manage."

"Of course," Andrew said. They had to trust to luck that they wouldn't have another winter like last year's never-ending snows. "Thank you, doctor."

"Good day to you, sir."

Andrew stood in the hall, staring after the physician. If only Steven could rally his spirits and try a little harder, there might be hope that Steven would keep the estate and Andrew could continue his insignificant existence in London.

A footman turned the corner. "Have you seen Mrs. Backus? There is a young lady in the sitting room to see her. A Miss—"

Andrew's head lolled back and he groaned. Miss Bentley! He'd forgotten his aunt had asked the Bentleys to come this morning with their eligible daughter. "She's in her room writing letters. Tell her I will be in shortly." And by shortly, he meant never. How to lose himself in this house? He would run for the orangery.

The footman bowed and continued to the stairs. Andrew

hurried down the corridor, but halted before he passed the open door to the sitting room. Miss Bentley was a pretty girl, if nothing else. He might like her if her parents were not intent on securing a proposal from him. He leaned carefully forward, but it was not dark curls that met his eye. Fiery red ones peeked out from under a deep green cap that matched her pelisse.

Andrew straightened. Miss Todd? With a chuckle, he slipped into the sitting room. His aunt was in for a surprise if she hoped for a private audience with the Bentleys.

"Miss Todd, what a pleasure to see you again." He bowed. Could he distract himself with Miss Todd when the others arrived? Mr. and Mrs. Bentley would not be happy to have their morning efforts thwarted by a stranger.

"I have come to pay my respects to your aunt," Miss Todd said through her curtsy. "I do not know if she will be happy to see me, as when last I was in Shropshire she seemed rather anxious for me to leave, but I cannot disrespect her by not paying a visit."

Andrew hid a guffaw behind his hand. No, Aunt Backus would not be pleased to see her here just as the Bentleys were expected. "I, for one, am glad you have come. She has planned a rather tedious morning."

Miss Todd raised an eyebrow. "More matchmaking attempts?" The winter wind had coaxed a shade of rosiness into her cheeks and nose, and the hem of her pelisse was wet from snow. Of course the Keppels would not keep a carriage. She must have walked.

"That is the only engagement in which anyone seems to participate whenever I am in the room," he said. "My aunt and the other ladies of Market Foxley think of nothing else."

She huffed. "How dreadful, to always be chased for one's fortune."

"You have no idea." Andrew grinned.

"This is true," she said, cocking her head. "I cannot say I have been chased by anyone other than my nurse as a child."

Andrew motioned to the sofa, and they both took their seats. "I can hardly believe that. Surely you have scores of suitors following you around London during the Season."

Miss Todd shook her head slowly, an ironic look in her eye. "I have never had a Season. My older sister was married only last February, and my parents would not spend the money to fit my wardrobe for London." She pulled at the sleeve of her pelisse. "This is my oldest sister's from three or four years ago. I had to remake it in a more modern style." She laughed, but was it because she truly found the situation humorous or because she wished to feign unconcern?

"I am sorry for it," Andrew said. "They are depriving London society of a most welcome addition."

She lowered her voice and leaned in. "Your aunt would not approve of you using such flirtation on someone not on her list of desired future nieces-in-law."

Heat rose to his face. He'd hardly meant to flirt. "I would appreciate your secrecy on the matter," he said, matching her hushed tone. "I rarely get the opportunity to exercise my skill in that area without it leading to yet another young lady out to catch me for herself."

She tilted her head towards him even further. "I will not tell a soul," she whispered.

What the deuce were her parents thinking to not put her into London society? She'd catch a husband at her first assembly, and they could return their focus to her other siblings. With a husband, she wouldn't have to wait for their attention to take her rightful place in Society.

The rattling of an approaching carriage jolted Andrew to his senses. He leaped to his feet. "That will be the Bentleys."

His aunt's voice carried in from the stairway. Dash it all, he should have given up the chance of speaking with Miss Todd and run for the orangery.

"If you will excuse me," he said, inching towards the corridor. "I'd best make myself scarce for this visit."

Footsteps sounded outside. A cool breeze trickled into the sitting room as the footman opened the door.

"The curtains!" Miss Todd cried. "Make haste." She darted around the sofa towards the heavy velvet curtains his aunt always hung in the winter.

Andrew scrambled after her, glancing behind him. This was absurd, but he hadn't any better option. The sounds of guests in the front hall grew louder. He dove behind the opposite curtain from Miss Todd and pressed himself against the wall. Across the window, she held in a giggle with her gloved hand.

"I do love this parlor," a woman said. "Can you imagine being mistress of this someday, Elizabeth?"

Miss Todd pulled a sour expression, and though he could only see half of her face for the curtain, Andrew had to choke down a laugh.

"I think he took a liking to you at the last assembly. You're halfway to the prize already."

Miss Todd's brow flew up, and she threw him a pointed look. Andrew scrunched his eyes closed and gave a swift shake of his head.

His aunt's voice from the other side of the room redirected that course of conversation, and after the exchange of greetings the furniture creaked as the party sat. Mrs. Bentley asked after the health of his uncle and brother.

Andrew tried to breathe shallowly so as not to move the thick, floor-length material encircling him. This was madness! How would his aunt not discover them, hiding in the curtains like naughty children?

"We had hoped to see Mr. Andrew Backus this morning," Mrs. Bentley said. "Is he at home?"

He cringed at the pause before his aunt spoke. "I heard him come down before me, but I did not see him in the passageway. I presume he has gone to the orangery, which is one of his favorite places in the house." Aunt Backus's clipped voice rang through the room. Despite the cool air rolling off the window, sweat trickled beneath Andrew's cravat. "Shall we retire to the orangery and find him there? We have some beautiful fruit nearly ripe."

Mrs. Bentley expressed enthusiastic delight, drowning out her daughter's demure acceptance of the plan. Thank the heavens. Andrew tried not to squirm as the group filed out of the sitting room.

After several moments, he poked his head around the edge of the curtain. The room had cleared. He blew out a long breath and extracted himself from the curtains.

"You are safe, Mr. Backus," Miss Todd said with a little giggle. She drew a swirl with the finger of her glove across the window, which had fogged in their hiding. How that had escaped his aunt's notice, Andrew would never know. Miss Todd's velvet cap had caught against the scratchy underside of the velvet curtains and fallen to one side.

"My aunt has discovered my usual hiding place." Before he knew what he did, Andrew reached out and righted the hat on her head.

Her hands flew to the brim, as though she hadn't noticed its misplacement. "I have no doubt you will find another one. And better."

"I enjoyed the orangery." He frowned. "It is warm, smells lovely, and has plenty of places to hide."

"Then might I suggest the stables the next time, which fit all your requirements except the lovely smell?"

A laugh burst from Andrew of its own accord at the impish twinkle in her eyes. "Thank you for saving my morning, Miss Todd. How shall I repay you?"

She waved a hand. "There is no repayment needed between friends."

"Then I have made a very fortunate friend." He offered her his arm. "Allow me to escort you outside while I make for the stables."

She took his arm lightly, not gripping it like many young ladies did. "Given the circumstances, I will call on your aunt some other time."

As the footman opened the door and they walked out into the wintry day, Andrew found that, for once in a very long time, he anticipated such a social call if it meant more laughs with Miss Todd. There would be no pressure for matchmaking in such a visit between friends.

Isabella could not help a smile as she made her way through the town. Half-timbered Tudor shops and houses lined the street, reflecting the soft November light. The church bell merrily chimed the hour from an ancient belfry, and her feet begged to skip the rest of the way to the bakery.

Despite missing the opportunity to make a better impression on his aunt, she counted the visit as a success. Several moments in intimate conversation, in which he looked completely at ease and in no way suspicious of her intentions—what more could she wish from a second encounter? His infectious laugh still trolled about her head.

Her hand rose to the brim of her cap. How quickly he'd reached to help her adjust it. A small gesture, but telling. She would lure and snap him up in the trap before he knew what had happened. This would be an easier conquest than she anticipated.

Hinwick's Bakery and Tea Shop came into view. She would not tell Aunt Keppel her ambitions. Though she loved the woman nearly as much as she loved her own sisters, she couldn't guess her aunt's response to the knowledge Isabella was chasing the uncatchable gentleman. Surely she would disapprove, especially when the Keppels' was a love match. Anyone lucky enough to secure such a marriage insisted on it being the only way to form an attachment.

Isabella put her hand on the door and paused. It wasn't as though she did not want a love match. Her parents had married for love, after all, though with how they had gone after husbands for their older daughters one would never have suspected that fact. They hardly mentioned it anymore.

Did it count as a love match if only one party held all the feelings? Isabella's aim was to earn Mr. Backus's affections. Perhaps in time she would form her own. With so easy a smile and quick a laugh, she could see herself coming to love him later. But she wouldn't worry over that now.

She pulled the door open and plunged into the warmth of the bakery. Aunt Keppel lifted her head from where she arranged buns behind the counter.

"Did you have a pleasant visit?" she asked.

Isabella bounded across the empty tea room. "Certainly. I should not be surprised to see him—them—again very soon."

Aunt Keppel watched her as she made her way to the back of the bakery. Though her aunt said nothing, a question burned in the stare. Isabella pulled off her cap and fished out the pins, which had done little in keeping the hat in place. But then, she hadn't attached them that morning knowing she would be jumping behind a great velvet curtain with Mr. Backus.

Yes, she had a very pleasant visit at Birchill Manor today. A few more visits such as that, and her parents would forget everything else in their raptures about her impending wedding.

Chapter Three

*H*ad fortune smiled on her again? Isabella pressed her nose against the window to make certain it was the Backus livery on the coach that passed. Yes, indeed! The black carriage stopped before the apothecary several doors down on the opposite side of the street.

Behind her, Aunt Keppel packaged gingerbread for a customer. Another waited for his turn at the counter. Isabella wouldn't bother her for help. She slid past the counter and into the back of the shop where her uncle worked at the steaming ovens. Mama and Papa warned her against appearing as a worker in the shop. Though she didn't see the harm in it—she had few genteel acquaintances in Market Foxley—she did not want to put her visits to the Keppels' at risk should they discover she'd been occupied in the kitchen or behind the counter.

"You're in a hurry," her uncle remarked as she snatched up paper and string.

She set them on the floured table and selected a few fingers of gingerbread from a basket. "I saw a friend in the street. I will repay you for the biscuits." She folded the stiff, brown paper around the treats. Mr. Backus would not notice the hasty wrapping, would he?

The weight of her uncle's hand on her shoulder stopped her in the middle of tying the string. "You may have as much gingerbread as you wish, my dear. No charge for family."

"I will eat you out of work if that is the case," she said with a laugh. "And these are not for me."

"They wouldn't happen to be for the gentleman you bumped into accidentally a few days ago, would they?"

A flush rose to her cheeks. Had Aunt Keppel said something about that? Isabella hadn't tried to see Mr. Backus again since her formal visit to Birchill last week, but he'd walked by the bakery Saturday, and she had to make the most of whatever situation fate granted. The slip on the ice had only been partially an act.

"Do what you must, I suppose." He winked and took up the peel to pull more loaves from the oven.

Isabella returned to her hasty tying. So much for keeping her intentions a secret. She ran upstairs for her cloak, boots, gloves, and reticule to hide the offering. Instead of using the front door and drawing more suspicion from Aunt Keppel, Isabella took the back door in the kitchen and hurried through the alleyway onto the street.

Good, the coach was still there. She had to think of something needed from the apothecary. Tooth powder for her aunt? Yes, it was a good enough excuse.

She crossed the slushy street, grateful she'd remembered to change her shoes. The wetness would have soaked through to her feet, and while she did not shrink from sacrificing to secure this match, she hoped not to fall ill from wet feet because of it.

Before she entered the apothecary's, she spied a face through the window of the Backuses' carriage. Though the glass warped her view of the occupant, she could not mistake the brown hair and dandyish neckcloth.

"Why, Mr. Backus!" She scurried to the coach. "How fortunate to meet you this morning."

Mr. Backus grinned and opened the window. "Another fine coincidence, Miss Todd. You are the best view I have seen today." His nose wrinkled. "My aunt has pulled me into visiting the Cowdens today. You must wish me luck."

"I take it Mrs. Cowden's daughter is not married."

"Neither of her two daughters is."

Isabella nearly giggled at his pout. "Is your aunt with the apothecary?"

Dejection clouded his usually bright eyes. "Yes, my brother

asked her to purchase a tincture," he said.

Isabella stepped closer. "How does he fare?"

"Last summer the doctor feared an early onset of rheumatism, as there was nothing else to explain the pain." Mr. Backus shook his head. "But I've hardly spoken to Steven since my return to know if that has changed. He prefers to keep to his room with the curtains drawn and extreme silence."

Isabella clasped her hands in front of her. How horrid, to be in such pain as to have no taste for sun or nature or company. "The poor man."

Mr. Backus mumbled his agreement.

"It must be a relief for him to have his brother back for a visit after you have lived so long in London," she suggested. This conversation had strayed into much more serious territory than their previous interactions.

"I do not know if he has noticed much difference."

"Surely a few moments to speak with his younger brother does not drain him terribly?" The hollowness in Mr. Backus's eyes tugged at her heart. He missed his brother's company. More than he feared the responsibility of inheritance, perhaps?

Mr. Backus shrugged. "I haven't tried very much. He did not open the door the first time I knocked, and I gave up my efforts after that."

"You should try again." She'd come so close to the carriage, she had to crane her neck to look at his face. "Retaining the friendship of siblings is well worth the effort." With her sisters married and brothers rarely home, the emptiness at Carnock House had become deafening. And on reunion, she found very little to say to her brothers or sisters, nor they to her. A gap had formed, though she did not know how.

"Perhaps. We shall see." Mr. Backus perked up. "But never mind that. My biggest worry now is how to evade the attentions of the Cowdens while in their lair. I tried everything I could to stay at home. My aunt would not hear of it."

Isabella reached into her reticule and pulled out the little packet of biscuits. "Perhaps this will sweeten the drudgery."

"Miss Todd, you are a dream," he said, wrapping his fingers around the package. He brought it to his nose. "Fresh gingerbread?"

"Baked this morning."

Mr. Backus gripped the window and ducked his head out of it as far as his shoulders would let him. "Are you engaged Friday evening? My aunt is hosting the Threshers, the Bentleys, the Cowdens, and the Hoggards for dinner. It will be unbearable. I wish you to be there."

Isabella smirked. "You tempt me beyond my ability to resist. What fun, to watch the marriage fox hunt!"

"Never mind that. Will you come? I shall send an invitation. It would be excruciating without a friend."

He called her a friend again. This was progress. Isabella pursed her lips as if considering, though she already knew her answer. This game she played was proving too simple. "Very well, I shall come. So long as you do not leave me to fend for myself while the fair maidens swarm you."

Mr. Backus grimaced. "As far as it is in my power, I shall be by your side the whole of the evening."

"Miss Todd."

Isabella whirled at the disapproving voice. Mrs. Backus! She curtsied regally to the older woman, who was wrapped in furs and fine wool. It wouldn't do to show fear or hesitation to this lady.

"You left before I could acknowledge your visit last week," Mrs. Backus said.

"I am very sorry, madam. I was needed at home, but I left my card." She hoped Mr. Backus could keep a straight expression behind her.

Mrs. Backus glanced at the bakery down the street and sniffed. "Yes. If I do not see you again before you leave, I do hope you enjoy your stay in Market Foxley. Good day to you."

Her nephew descended from the coach to hand his aunt

into it. "Friday evening," he mouthed before re-entering.

Isabella bit her lips. Little did Mrs. Backus know she would be seeing quite a lot of Isabella during her visit. She had sensed a dislike in the older woman on previous stays. Perhaps the untamable red in her hair offended the lady as it did Mama. She could not think of anything she had done to affront her.

As the coach pulled away, Mr. Backus threw her a conspiring grin. Isabella's chest swelled with satisfaction. She'd gained one more step on the road to victory.

Andrew slipped the string from the brown paper in his lap and pulled out a biscuit. At least he had Miss Todd's company to look forward to on Friday. "I'd forgotten about Hinwick's bakery. Why do we never order from them?"

"I prefer Smith's on the other side of town."

"But they don't have gingerbread," Andrew said, holding out the packet to her. Aunt Backus shook her head. He pulled it back. More for him.

She watched the gingerbread travel to his mouth. "I did not know you liked gingerbread."

In truth, neither had he. But the fine blend of spicy sweetness felt perfect for the cold weather. "How long must we stay at the Cowdens'?"

Aunt Backus laced her fingers together and settled them firmly on her knees. Andrew stopped chewing. This could not end well.

"Andrew, it is time you started acting the part of an heir."

His shoulders slumped. This again. He attempted to swallow the half-chewed gingerbread, but started choking. He coughed into his sleeve, his aunt remaining silent until he had recovered himself.

"Part of those duties is attending to the families in the neighborhood. And it would do you great service to find a wife from among their daughters."

Andrew cleared his throat against the remaining crumbs. "I am not the heir, and therefore have no reason to give up bachelorhood yet." The one thousand pounds and small piece of property currently promised him in the will would do well enough for an unmarried gentleman.

His aunt sighed long-sufferingly. "As of yet, you are not the heir. But you have more the capacity to perform expected duties than your brother. Your Uncle Backus is warming to the idea. He sees its sense." Uncertainty flashed across her grim expression, but disappeared in a moment. "We do not know how long we have to prepare before the estate is passed on."

"You cannot just take the estate from Steven." He fought to keep the heat from his voice. "He was brought up to be heir. I was brought up for a life of ease and dependence on whoever will sponsor my lavish habits."

Aunt Backus did not smile at his ridiculous words. He'd said them with too much force to do the teasing justice.

"If Steven cannot marry, the estate will pass to you in the end. Why not begin with giving it to you, that you may dedicate your life to its upkeep and improvement?"

Andrew winced. How awful that sounded, devoting every moment to a drafty old house and dreary family reputation. "I know very little of how to be an heir."

"If you remained at Birchill regularly for longer than a few weeks, rather than whenever it suited your fancy, perhaps we could teach you."

There was no winning. Andrew settled back to munch on more gingerbread. Steven would get well eventually. He had to. Then their aunt and uncle would release Andrew from this pressure. "I invited Miss Todd to our dinner on Friday."

Aunt Backus threw up her hands. "Miss Todd? Of all people, Miss Todd."

"She is young, female, and unattached," Andrew said. "Just the sort of person with whom you wish me to associate."

"Yes, from an upstart family with no respect for propriety," Aunt Backus growled.

"The Todds have been in the gentry for generations. As have the Keppels." Surely Miss Todd's grandfather would not have disowned Mr. Keppel the baker if they had only recently ascended the social ladder.

Aunt Backus did not answer, but turned away from him. Was it the relation to a baker that made her hate Miss Todd so? He couldn't account for it.

"I am sending an invitation this afternoon," he prodded.

"I wish you would not."

Andrew wrapped the remaining gingerbread and tucked it into his coat pocket. "If I am to act as heir, do I not then get to invite my choice of guests to our parties?"

It earned him a glare icier than Birchill's frozen stream. After a long while she spoke. "Very well. Though I will not stand for you giving her the entirety of your attention that night."

"Of course not." But he had first promised Miss Todd not to leave her side, and did that not trump any promise he made afterward? He would have to bring her along in paying respect to each of the young ladies. Miss Thresher would love that.

And for once, he found the prospect of seeing that young lady's face enticing, if only to see envy clearly written all over it as he paraded about with Miss Todd.

Chapter Four

ell played, Aunt.

Andrew sat back in his chair near the fire between his aunt and Mrs. Hoggard. Miss Todd sat across the room at the pianoforte, playing her fingers to the bone and singing herself hoarse at Aunt Backus's request. Twice she had called for Miss Todd to play another song, though she hardly gave the music a listening ear. She was too intent on pushing Andrew into conversation with Miss Hoggard, who sat beside her mother.

"Miss Hoggard, have you seen our terrace?" Aunt Backus asked the daughter, who kept throwing shy glances in Andrew's direction. "It is a veritable fairyland in the winter. Our gardener keeps many varieties of winter-hardy plants throughout the garden, and I believe tonight he has even lit the lanterns."

"It sounds like a dream," Miss Hoggard said, her voice so breathy Andrew struggled to understand it.

"Would Mr. Backus give you a tour?" the mother asked.

Andrew put up his hands. "I must protest. Miss Hoggard would catch her death from the cold."

Miss Todd's song ended to a half-hearted ovation. He avoided Miss Thresher's indignant glare from the other circle of guests as he applauded the performance. His aunt would give her a proper turn at him, he had no doubt.

Aunt Backus leaned over the arm of her chair. "Do play one more for us, my dear."

Another? Andrew inwardly groaned as Miss Todd nodded. It made perfect sense that she wished to put herself on good terms with his aunt, but everyone in the room could see his aunt's meddling. If only Steven were here to draw some of her notice, but he did not know the last time Steven attended a dinner.

Miss Todd arranged another book of music on the stand of the instrument. If this kept on, Andrew would retire with pains as convincing as Steven's. He had invited Miss Todd solely as an escape from the inheritance chasers. It had done him little good so far. Earlier Aunt Backus had seated Miss Todd on the opposite end of the dinner table from him, and he'd hardly spoken two words to the young lady during the course of the evening.

"Oh, Jane can survive a little chill," Mrs. Hoggard said. Never mind that she had positioned them in the secluded corner by the fire because "Miss Hoggard must be kept warm for her health."

"Mr. Backus, will you assist me?"

His heart leaped at the voice that carried across the room. Finally, Miss Todd came to his rescue. He jumped from his chair, ignoring his aunt's objections and Mrs. Hoggard's stutters of surprise, and hurried to the pianoforte. "Shall I turn pages for you?"

Miss Todd lifted her face to regard him, and for a moment his breath caught. The curve of her lips, the sparkle in her green eyes, the way her copper curls softly framed her face—she was a masterpiece.

"Miss Thresher and Miss Cowden were just talking about how well you sing," she said. "My voice has tired. Will you sing for me?"

What was this strange sensation in his chest, like the thrill of racing a gig down a straight country lane at full speed with the wind tugging his clothes and hair? "What am I to sing?"

She went back to the music before her, breaking the spell. Its effects lingered in the air between them, as disorienting as a morning mist.

"I thought to play *Greensleeves*. I trust you recall the words."

Who didn't know that old song? "I shall try my best to do them justice." If he could remember how to sing after that odd encounter.

Miss Todd returned her fingers to the keys casually, as if she practiced alone in her own parlor instead of drawing envious glares from every unmarried female in the room. The introduction filled the mostly silent chamber before Andrew began.

"Alas, my love, you do me wrong
To cut me off discourteously;
For I have loved you so long,
Delighting in your company."

The light purple skirts of her gown fluttered as she kept time with her slipper. Andrew stumbled over the entrance to the chorus, and she joined in without a hint of the tiredness she claimed.

"Greensleeves was all my joy,
Greensleeves was my delight,
Greensleeves was my heart of gold,
And who but my lady Greensleeves?"

They continued through the song, Miss Todd joining in on each chorus. He enjoyed the way their voices mixed, especially when Miss Todd threw in unexpected lines of harmony. Much like she had added that unanticipated spark of amusement to his life since he'd arrived in Market Foxley.

As the final notes of the melody faded, Aunt Backus clapped loudly. "You did very well, Miss Todd. Miss Bentley, would you favor us with a song?"

Andrew offered Miss Todd his arm and helped her to her feet. She sent him a covert grin. They had thwarted his aunt's plans, and although his aunt bid him turn Miss Bentley's pages as he escorted Miss Todd to a seat, he would not count the night as a disaster. Having a friend such as Miss Todd was turning out more pleasurable than he anticipated.

Andrew faltered back a step when Steven opened his door Saturday morning. He'd knocked so lightly, he assumed his brother would not hear even if awake.

"Yes?" The corners of Steven's eyes pulled tight, evidence of the continued pain.

"I…I wished only to see how you got on this morning."

"As well as any morning." Steven's gaze fell to the ground. "You may come in, if you would like."

Andrew followed him into the darkened room and took a seat in the brightest spot near the window. Beyond a brief greeting upon his arrival from London, he hadn't spoken to his brother like this in months. Steven stiffly crossed the room to sit on the edge of the bed. He rubbed his knees once seated.

"How are you enjoying your stay?" Steven asked.

"As well as could be expected." Andrew twiddled his thumbs. He hadn't thought of what to say. They'd been the best of friends all their lives, until the younger brother left for a permanent stay in London and the older contracted this insufferable ailment. Why did Andrew find it so hard to make conversation?

Steven stretched his back when he'd finished with his knees. "There was a dinner party last night." With his room so near to the drawing room, he must have heard quite a lot.

"Yes, Aunt Backus invited a few neighbors." Did Steven know of her matchmaking efforts? Or her plans for the will?

"Anyone of interest?"

Andrew swallowed. Yes, one person of particular interest. "The Threshers, the Bentleys, the Cowdens, and the Hoggards. As well as a Miss Todd, who is staying with her aunt and uncle for Christmas."

Steven nodded. "Fine young ladies."

Andrew avoided his gaze. "It was enjoyable enough. But nothing like dinners in London." He rose, rubbing his hands on the front of his trousers. "I'd best be going. I'm certain you want rest."

"Did I hear you singing after dinner?" Steven asked as Andrew made his way to the door.

Andrew laughed. "Yes, Miss Todd pulled me into it, or I would not have sung in front of this party. Too many who wish to draw my good will with flattery." The words came out quicker than he could rein them in. In their younger days, Steven liked to tease him about his enjoyment of singing, to the point Andrew rarely sang anymore. He left it to the young ladies to perform for compliments.

"Miss Todd must have been very convincing." For a moment the discomfort faded from Steven's eyes as he scrutinized his brother.

Andrew's neck warmed beneath his collar.

"Do you like Miss Todd?" Steven asked. "I have only met her once or twice."

Like her? Andrew balked at the question. His bizarre reaction to Miss Todd's upturned face at the pianoforte last night was hardly a good indication. The tension in the room because of his aunt's efforts surely put him in a weak position. Did he like Miss Todd? Of course. As much as he liked any of the young ladies among his set of friends in London. Though none of them would have dragged him into singing so easily as Miss Todd had. That had more to do with Miss Todd's ways and manners than anything.

At the very most, his heart was only one quarter gone, and that was almost nothing. He'd given a quarter of his heart to plenty of young women, and any silly thoughts or fancies quickly dissolved. No one ever piqued his interest enough to give away his heart completely. Bachelorhood continued to hold the majority of his admiration.

So he harbored a little fondness for Miss Todd. It meant nothing. And Steven would not ferret out this secret. Not that it was much of a secret.

"She is a good sort of young lady, I suppose," Andrew said, lifting a shoulder. "She doesn't put on airs like Miss Thresher, nor is she timid like Miss Hoggard. She makes a good addition to the company."

"Is she pretty?"

Time to go. "Pretty enough. I hope you will have the chance to renew your acquaintance one of these days to judge for yourself." And to satisfy any more curiosity without forcing Andrew into statements that could be construed as evidence to feelings that were not there. Or mostly weren't there and would soon fade. "Can I have anything sent up for you?"

Steven shook his head, and Andrew turned to leave.

"Andrew?"

He paused and glanced over his shoulder.

"Thank you for coming." Steven looked so thin, sitting on his bed in a banyan wrapped too tightly with the curtains closed and fire dim.

Andrew smiled. "I'm glad I did." He closed the door behind him. The chill in his heart at seeing his brother so undone from the man he used to be melted at Steven's parting words. One more thing for which he owed Miss Todd his gratitude.

Gracious, that list was getting incredibly long.

Chapter Five

*M*r. Backus sat across the little table from Isabella, stirring his coffee with a stick of gingerbread. "And then the headmaster rounded the corner. You can imagine his face when he saw the mess. Feathers everywhere."

She covered her face. "Oh, that is horrid! You must have looked a sight." Aunt Keppel had already brought them new drinks and a fresh plate of sweets since Mr. Backus arrived unannounced at the bakery that afternoon. But whether he avoided someone or sought out her company, Isabella could not decide.

"I think we frightened the poor man." He went to take a bite out of his gingerbread, but it had been soaking so long the end fell off and plopped back into his coffee. Isabella laughed as he stared after it.

The tea room had cleared several minutes ago when an older woman and her younger companion left. Even with the audience, Mr. Backus had spoken more at his leisure than Isabella had ever heard in company. At dinner the week before, he had gone sullen and quiet in the midst of so many people vying for his attention. This afternoon he seemed much more like the London version of himself she'd heard so much talk of—vibrant, humorous, carefree.

Movement out the window caught her eye, and her spirits plummeted. What a way to end a fine afternoon. "Miss Thresher!" she cried.

Mr. Backus startled, turning to stare at the young woman marching across the street towards Hinwick's. "Where shall I go?"

Isabella snatched his hat and coat from the table beside

them and shoved them into his arms. "Hurry, out the back through the kitchens." Miss Thresher had almost made it to the door.

Mr. Backus sprinted for the back of the room and rolled awkwardly over the top of the counter instead of circumventing it. He collapsed behind the counter with a string of grunts. A moment later his head popped up over the wooden surface.

Well, if he wanted to be dramatic. Isabella shook her head and waved him towards the kitchen door. If Miss Thresher heard the shuffling as he crawled towards the back, what an awkward situation they'd find themselves in.

The door banged open and Isabella whirled. "Ah, Miss Thresher. What a pleasant surprise." She curtsied.

Miss Thresher returned the gesture with a stiff and hurried one of her own. "Did I see Mr. Backus through the window?"

Isabella looked around the tea room. His cup still sat on the table, but no other evidence remained of his presence. "No, I believe you are mistaken. My uncle was taking some refreshment before returning to work."

Miss Thresher's lip curled. "I am not so much a fool as to confuse a baker for a gentleman."

"But when the baker is a gentleman, the confusion is understandable." Isabella gave a tight-lipped smile. Her uncle was the son of a gentleman, even if he lacked the fortune to prove it.

Miss Thresher did not respond, but surveyed the tea room. At the back, Aunt Keppel came forward from the kitchen with eyebrows raised.

"Tea," Miss Thresher called, then settled herself at a table. "We have not had much opportunity to speak since your arrival, Miss Todd."

Thank the stars. Isabella slowly sank into the chair across from Miss Thresher and folded her hands firmly in her lap. Would Mr. Backus wait in the kitchens until his pursuer had gone? They hadn't said a proper goodbye.

Aunt Keppel brought a steaming cup of tea, and Miss

Thresher did not so much as look at her. "You seem to have taken a liking to Mr. Backus," the other young lady said.

Smiles. All smiles. "I think you misconstrue our acquaintance. We are friends, in the same manner as he is friends with you or Miss Bentley."

"And yet, any time I see him in town, you happen to be with him." Miss Thresher wrapped her thin fingers around the handle of the cup. "The book shop, the apothecary, the haberdasher's. I do not think I have seen him once without you also being in attendance."

Miss Thresher was more astute than she appeared. "I find it interesting that you also appear at those same moments," Isabella said. "What a coincidence that three friends should show up in the exact place at the same time. Most would call that good fortune. Though I assure you, I never meet him otherwise."

"I should warn you about Mr. Andrew Backus," Miss Thresher said, raising her cup. "He is a cad and a fop who will lead along respectable young ladies, only to abandon them with their reputations tarnished beyond repair."

My, what bitterness. "Such a way to speak of one's friends!" She hoped Mr. Backus remained to listen to this. They would laugh about it later.

Miss Thresher glowered over her drink, fingers squeezing as though to break the handle. "You will be sorry if you do not heed my words. Mr. Backus will break your heart as fast as he has won it. He is not the marrying sort. Any upstanding young lady would do well to avoid him, my dear."

Isabella leaned forward, unsure if her words would come out as a snicker or a hiss. "Then why do you chase him like a hawk in pursuit of a field mouse?"

Miss Thresher took a drink, then choked on the hot liquid. She practically dropped the cup, sending it sloshing all over the table.

"It is no secret in this town on whom Miss Thresher has set her eyes," Isabella said. "Perhaps you should listen to your own advice, *my dear.*"

The sputtering Miss Thresher flew out of her seat. "What is this rancid drink? I will not pay for that. Not one farthing!"

Isabella closed her eyes and drew in a slow breath. Only one dark spot had tainted her time in Market Foxley. This young lady. "I will add it to your tab," she said sweetly.

"Take heed, Miss Todd." And with that, Miss Thresher turned on her heel and stormed out of the bakery.

Isabella blinked as the door rattled shut. Unbearable girl. She wandered back to the kitchen, taking Miss Thresher's rejected cup of tea with her. Uncle Keppel met her with a knowing grin.

"Is Mr. Backus still here?" She didn't need to ask, as her aunt and uncle were the only ones in the kitchen. Unless Mr. Backus had gone above to their living quarters, which she doubted.

"No, but he was brushing flour from his trousers and sleeves as he went."

She laughed at the image of a dandy like Mr. Backus covered in flour and running for his life. No matter what Miss Thresher said, Mr. Backus was no cad and only a little of a fop. Perhaps he loved the frivolous things of the world too much, but who among the gentry didn't?

Still, a weight settled over her heart at Miss Thresher's caution. She'd become too comfortable with Mr. Backus. If she did not take care, he would know her plot. And an attraction on her part had no place in that aim.

"Is something wrong?" her aunt asked.

Isabella smiled and shook her head, then made her way upstairs. She did still want this, did she not? Attaching herself to a flighty husband for the sake of gaining her parents' notice, in addition to a comfortable fortune, was worth the sacrifice. She walked into this situation with both eyes wide open, knowing what sort of husband Mr. Backus would make. It would do her no good to hope that he would become something more.

Aunt Backus waited for Andrew at the door when he arrived at Birchill Manor, flour still coating his knees and sticking to the arms of his jacket.

"Where were you?"

Andrew removed his hat and coat and handed them to the footman. "I…"

"Did you forget we were to drink tea with Mrs. Cowden and her daughters?"

Yes, he'd purposefully forgotten. "Oh, I am sorry. I thought that was tomorrow."

Aunt Backus's rigid lips told him she did not believe his lie for one moment. "I do not have to ask where you were."

Andrew shuffled past her, color draining from his face. "I needed a—"

"Ginger biscuit and cup of tea from Hinwick's Bakery," she finished for him.

"Coffee, as it were." He smiled innocently.

"Honestly, Andrew. You disdain the suggestion of marriage and spurn every girl in the town, and yet you allow the one young lady we consider unsuitable for your attention to ensnare you with barely the lift of a finger."

Andrew halted, scowling. "Unsuitable? Miss Todd is hardly unsuitable."

Aunt Backus's hands flew to her hips. "And where is she staying?" Her eyes raked his jacket and trousers. "In the home of a tradesman."

"Mr. Keppel was a gentleman, and his family are still respected members of the gentry." The front hall suddenly grew too warm for comfort. "Miss Todd has a handsome dowry. Her father boasts a larger and longer-established estate than Birchill. And what's more…" He straightened his waistcoat. "Miss Todd is not pursuing me like every other female in this neighborhood. We can enjoy one another's company without the expectation of something more. Is it so very wrong of me to seek out the companionship of someone by whom I do not feel threatened?" He made for the stairs. If Aunt Backus insisted on forcing him to consider marriage, perhaps he should return to London sooner than planned.

"Not trying to catch you? Ha! That girl is trying to catch you as surely as anyone else in Market Foxley, and you have fallen for her antics. The little vixen."

Andrew spun before he got to the stairs. Aunt Backus stood with her hand to her forehead as though his perceived stupidity had given her a headache.

"I do not know why you abhor Miss Todd," he growled, "but rest assured I will not make any offer for her hand. Nor will I offer for Miss Thresher, Miss Bentley, either of the Miss Cowdens, or Miss Hoggard. I will leave for London come January as single as when I arrived. Try as you might, my mind will not change."

Then he stormed up the stairs, with Aunt Backus's shouted disapprovals echoing after him.

Chapter Six

※

*I*sabella thanked the farmer's son as he transferred eggs from his basket to hers. Aunt Keppel had been detained, and while Papa had explicitly said Isabella was not to be seen working in the front of the shop, bringing in the deliveries at the back door would not overstep her promise. No one could see her from here.

She handed the boy, perhaps eleven or twelve years old, the payment with a little wrapped parcel of biscuits. A grin spread across his face. "Thank you, miss." He pocketed the coins, but kept the treat in one hand. "Oh, I nearly forgot. This is for you."

Isabella cocked her head as the boy drew out a card and handed it to her. "Thank you."

The words "Andrew Backus, Birchill Manor" scrolled across the front. Mr. Backus's card? She turned it over to find a hastily written message, slightly smeared, on the back.

She nodded gratefully to the boy, bid him good day, and hurried into the bakery. After setting the eggs beside the table, she mounted the stairs to her room, fearful of her aunt and uncle's questions. The room was tiny compared to the one she occupied at home, and it took three steps to cross to the window. She held the card up to the light.

Miss Todd,

Tomorrow Mr. Jacobs and Mr. Nicholas are coming to Birchill for sledge races, and my aunt has invited every young lady in fifty miles. Will you come to ward them off?

— A.B.

Isabella rested her brow on the cold glass of the window, shutting her eyes against the brightness of the sun that peeked over the rooftops. Inside, her heart flitted this way and that like a bonnet ribbon caught in a playful breeze. Sledge racing! She'd never seen it before. Would they let the ladies participate? She hoped so.

Leave it to Mr. Backus to surprise her once again. With a girlish giggle, she kissed the card.

She froze, lips against the paper. What was she doing? Dolt. This was not to be a love match just yet. She had to secure him before she thought of silly things.

Isabella walked serenely to her bed and buried the card under her pillow, trying with all her power to rein in the excitement bubbling over at the thought of tomorrow's escapade.

Andrew grinned and hurried down the front steps as the Hoggards' carriage pulled up the lane. A fine dusting of powdery snow had settled on the estate the night before, making him fear for the party. But the weather cleared that morning and left everything in pristine condition for the day's events. A thin layer of clouds veiled the sun, but no further storms threatened.

The footman opened the coach door, and Mrs. Hoggard descended, followed by her daughter. Andrew nodded his greeting and stepped past them. He waved away the footman, offering his hand into the carriage. A slender glove grasped it. A green velvet sleeve appeared as he helped her down, followed by a pair of bright eyes. Today she wore a white stole over her pelisse and carried a matching muff. Wise, as it would get cold in the sledge.

"Miss Todd, I am pleased you could make it," he said as they moved aside to let Mr. Hoggard out.

"I wouldn't miss sledge races, to be certain." Her voice skipped lightly through the chill air.

From the front door, Aunt Backus cast them a disapproving glare, one he hoped Miss Todd failed to see.

He looped her hand around his elbow. "Come, we're all

gathered in the orangery. You will be my companion in the first race." He had unfortunately promised his aunt to allow the other young ladies turns to be his companions. A compromise for his aunt allowing Miss Todd to come.

"We get to ride out with you?" Her fingers tightened on his arm.

"Of course!" Andrew said as they approached his aunt. "I would never leave you behind."

His insistence made Aunt Backus's eyebrows shoot up nearly to her receding hairline. Andrew winced. Perhaps that had been a little too enthusiastic for his aunt's ears. Miss Todd wouldn't take it as seriously as it sounded.

His partner greeted Aunt Backus, earning only a frigid reply, before he whisked her off to the cosy orangery. They wove through the vibrant greenery to find the rest of the group. Miss Todd ran her fingers along the sunny fruit as they passed. He led her over to his friends, who had just returned from Cambridge.

"Miss Todd, may I introduce you to my friends, Mr. Nicholas and Mr. Jacobs."

Nicholas gave him a sly look as he bowed handsomely to Miss Todd. Jacobs was not so discreet. "A lady, Backus? I thought you attempted to avoid those."

Andrew laughed to prevent a groan. *Dash it all, Jacobs. It isn't like that.* "She is staying in Market Foxley through the Christmas season and has graciously agreed to join our party."

"Perhaps Miss Todd would like to accompany me on the first run," Nicholas said gallantly. "My sledge is, after all, the fastest."

Andrew bristled. The knave, trying to prance in and—

"I am already engaged to ride with Mr. Backus," Miss Todd said, throwing Nicholas a coy glance. "But perhaps on the next round."

Andrew quickly led her out of the orangery to avoid any more flirting from Nicholas. Grooms already worked to hitch horses to the two-person sledges, which were little more than gigs fitted with runners instead of wheels.

"Nicholas thinks his sledge is the swiftest, but really they are quite identical." He didn't know why he felt the need to defend his to Miss Todd. "The same coach maker built them last year after the Ackermann's article on the royal sledge party in Europe. The article made sledges all the rage in this town."

"We certainly had the winter last year to take advantage." Miss Todd walked around to the opposite side of the sledge, observing the workmanship. "It seems light and fast."

Andrew folded his arms and leaned them against the side. "It is breathtakingly fast." A slight stretch. But the eager widening of her eyes was worth it.

"Shall we start?" Nicholas called. "The sooner I win, the sooner Miss Todd rides with me." He shot Andrew a wicked smile.

Scoundrel. Nicholas was clearly trying to gauge Andrew's feelings. Well, Andrew would disappoint him, as Nicholas would find very little for all his efforts.

Andrew helped Miss Todd onto the seat of the sledge and climbed in the other side. Servants brought out thick wool and fur blankets to keep them warm, and his companion buried her hands in her muff. In the other sledges, Nicholas aided the younger Miss Cowden while Jacobs assisted a disgruntled Miss Thresher.

Mr. Bentley stood to the side. "You will race to the hermitage, down the eastern lane, around the manor, and back to this spot. Is everyone ready?"

He brought his hand down to signal the start and cheers erupted behind them. Andrew urged his dapple grey gelding forward to the music of Miss Todd's laughter. In no time, the crisp wind nipped at their cheeks. Bare trees streaked by in thin, black lines against the snowy landscape. Their horse's breath trailed in clouds behind him, the tune of the little bells that chimed from his harness echoing in the stillness.

"Faster!" Miss Todd called. "Mr. Nicholas will catch us."

She leaned forward, as though it would help the horse keep them ahead of the other sledges.

Nicholas and Miss Cowden pulled even with them, and his friend tipped his hat before cracking the whip and gaining the lead. Andrew glanced at Miss Todd. Her eyes fixed on the other sledge and her mouth pulled into a determined line. He chuckled under his breath.

"Never fear. We shall catch them," he said.

They approached the bridge over Birchill Stream, which was frozen and covered in a thick layer of snow. Andrew tried to coax his horse faster to cut Nicholas off, but his friend would not let him in. Nicholas slowed to take the bridge.

Miss Todd grabbed his arm before he could pull back. "Can we go over the ice?"

"Well, yes, but—"

"Take it!" She pointed, still watching Nicholas on the bridge. "We'll steal the lead."

Andrew tightened the left reins, wheeling the horse around and setting it on a path for the gently sloping bank. The gelding hesitated, but Andrew urged it forward. The ice was thick. It would hold.

Miss Todd leaned out of the sledge, watching the ice go by. To their right, Nicholas quit the bridge and picked up speed.

"Hurry," she said, leaning farther towards their opponents, "they're getting away!"

She was too far out. "Miss Todd, if you would—"

The sledge hit a bump coming up the opposite bank and the vehicle careened to one side. With a shriek, Miss Todd tumbled out into the snow.

Andrew shouted her name, throwing his weight to the other side of the sledge to keep it from completely turning over. He desperately pulled on the reins. The frightened horse refused to slow for what seemed an age. Andrew's roaring pulse drowned out the gelding's pitiful braying.

Finally he got the sledge stopped and leaped over the side.

"Miss Todd!" A sliver of green velvet poked out from over the bank.

Idiot. Fool. He should have waited for the bridge. Andrew ran, the snow pulling at his boots and impeding his haste. *All that is holy, please let her not be injured.* She lay on her side, partially buried in the whiteness.

He dropped to his knees and fell forward on his hands to see her face. "Miss Todd?" *Please be well. Please be well. Please be well.*

She groaned and rolled over on her back, brushing snow from her face. "A fine sledge partner I am," she grumbled. "Can't even stay in the sledge." Then she giggled.

Andrew let out a long breath. "Are you hurt?" He leaned back, giving her room to sit up with his assistance.

"Not terribly. My pride worst of all. That devil is going to win the race."

Andrew snorted and shook his head. He adjusted his feet under him, then wrapped his arms around her and pulled her up with him. The faintest whiff of ginger and cinnamon hit his nose as she steadied herself against him. He halted, Miss Todd still in his arms.

She regarded him, one eyebrow lifted. Snowflakes clung to her hair like morning dew. The fall had properly mussed her carefully laid ringlets, and little beads of melted snow shone from her lashes. Brisk air had given her cheeks a tantalizing rosiness.

Or perhaps it was their closeness.

Andrew was practically pressing her against his chest.

His arms instantly dropped, and he stepped back, clearing his throat. "Are you sure you are not hurt? I cannot return you to your aunt and uncle like this."

"Oh. Yes." Miss Todd fretted with the skirts of her coat and walked stiffly over to retrieve her muff a few paces away. "No, I think I am well. I shall be sore in the morning, but nothing is very wrong."

The knots in Andrew's stomach still pinched. "I shall send for the doctor when we return."

Miss Todd shook her head violently, scrambling towards the sledge. "I am well. Hurry, if we cannot defeat Mr. Nicholas, we can still beat Mr. Jacobs!"

Andrew ran a hand over his face, but it did little to slow his pounding heart. Insane woman. She could have been killed or seriously injured, and here she wanted to finish the race. He waded back to the sledge. Miss Todd had already pulled herself in, readjusting the blankets over her lap.

"Come!" She snatched his arm and tugged him reluctantly in. Bells jingled behind them. Jacobs must have been delayed for them to still have a chance.

Andrew took the reins and turned to his companion, who had sidled up closer than before. He fought the urge to lift his arm and drape it around her shoulders. "You are the craziest young lady I have ever met."

She didn't answer. Only threw him an impish grin that melted away any other scolding he'd hoped to give.

At that moment, two things struck him, as shocking as snow dropped from a buckling branch onto an unsuspecting passerby. The first: an overwhelming desire to kiss those full, grinning lips. The second...

"Make haste! They will catch us," she cried.

Andrew prodded the horse forward, blocking the way of Jacobs and a sour-faced Miss Thresher. He gradually brought the sledge back up to speed, the cool wind laughing at his dilemma.

His second realization he found far harder to swallow. But with Miss Todd warm and smiling against his side and his breath refusing to slow, lest he miss another chance at inhaling her spicy scent, he had no choice but to admit that his heart was most definitely half gone.

Isabella slipped between her blankets, which Aunt Keppel had just heated with the warming pan, and sighed. The heat slowly seeped into her frozen limbs, which she'd worried would never feel warm again after she'd dumped herself into the snow earlier.

She rolled to her side, pulling the blankets closer, and rubbed her aching shoulder. Perhaps she should have told her aunt about the fall. But what if her aunt and uncle refused to let her participate again? If Mr. Backus held another such party, she had to attend. She could not afford to lose any opportunity to secure that gentleman's attention. Christmas was only two weeks away, and she was expected in London soon after. If her parents remembered to send for her. They'd forgotten before. Perhaps they would decide to extend their stay in Town and finally allow her a Season. Though, she might not need one by then.

The dying fire crackled softly from the hearth, the only light left in the dark bedroom. She hugged her arms around herself. What if Mr. Backus did not take her bait? He had sounded so frustrated with her after the accident. And yet, the intensity in his eyes and the way his gaze traveled over her lips when he'd returned to the sledge…those things had to mean something, did they not? He hadn't pulled away when she moved close to him.

She fingered the end of her braid. He looked like a man considering love in that moment, but could it all have come from fear over the fall? Or perhaps he sought some amusement while he had to stay in Market Foxley, and decided to find it in the visiting lady? Many men pretended to have such feelings for the fun of it.

Isabella flopped onto her back, sending a wave of soreness up her left side. What stupidity, leaning that far out of the sledge. Was she being equally stupid in continuing her pursuit of Mr. Backus? Deep down, she could not deny her attachment to his easy smile and friendly manners. If he proved to only be playing a game, the ache would pierce far greater than this soreness.

As she let herself drift into the forgetfulness of sleep, she could not help but wonder who was really playing with whom in this silly game of attraction.

Chapter Seven

❦

*I*sabella smoothed flour over the rolling pin. Her current state would horrify her parents if they could see her just now. But Papa had only instructed she not get caught working in the front of the shop. If no one saw her, she'd not be disobeying his wishes.

Her uncle had gone for eggs when the farmer's son did not show that morning, and her aunt sought out material for new tea towels. They'd briefly closed the shop, so Isabella did not fear discovery of her efforts to replenish the dangerously short supply of gingerbread. With no one around to do the work, she might as well repay her aunt and uncle for their kindness to her.

Isabella sectioned off the dough and dumped a portion onto the table. Mixing the dough had tired her arms, but thank the heavens the soreness from Tuesday's fall had mostly disappeared. She patted down the red-brown mixture, then moved the rolling pin back and forth in even strokes across it as her aunt had shown her years ago.

The bell above the shop's front door rang, and she froze mid roll. Aunt Keppel couldn't have returned yet, and Uncle Keppel would have come through the back door. A customer. Did they not see the sign indicating the bakery was closed?

"Hello?" a masculine voice called.

She could sneak out the back door. Making her way up the creaky stairs to the living quarters would only alert him.

The thick heels of boots clopped across the tea room. Dash it all, as Mr. Backus would say. A chill ran down her spine, despite the sweat that beaded on her brow from the heat of the ovens behind her. She gripped the rolling pin in one hand and scanned the room for the poker. If it was a thief come to take her uncle and aunt's hard-earned money... What? She would clobber him with a rolling pin? Isabella cringed and caught up the poker. Perhaps the sight of her prepared for him would scare him off.

The footsteps carried past the counter. Isabella backed into a corner, waiting for the sound of someone rummaging around.

"Miss Todd?"

Good heavens, she knew that voice. Her cheeks flushed as a handsome smile popped around the corner.

"There you are. I was just trying to avoid Mrs. Hoggard in the street. Do you mind..." Mr. Backus glanced from the extended rolling pin to the poker and back to her face. "Is everything all right?"

"Yes, of course." She tried to laugh as she leaned the poker against the hearth. "I was helping my aunt."

"Is that it?" His brows stayed raised.

"I sometimes help her bake biscuits." She wanted to run for the door. Why had she assumed the worst? Now she'd made a fool of herself in front of the one man she couldn't afford to.

"With the poker."

Isabella flashed him a smile as she took up her task again. "I was stoking the fire." Her dry throat scratched as she spoke. She had no way out of this one. Here she was, doing lower class work after threatening him with a poker and rolling pin. What he must think of her. "I apologize. I am not fit for company."

He would turn on his heel and march out of the shop. She kept her eyes on the dough. He knew who her aunt and uncle were. If he found issue with her helping them, then perhaps he was all the terrible things Miss Thresher warned about. Isabella would be better off without someone like that. And still, her face stayed red as a holly berry.

A flash of brown, then one of blue caught the corner of her eye. "May I be of service?" Mr. Backus had removed his greatcoat and jacket to drape over a nearby chair, and now rolled up the soft linen of his sleeves.

"I suppose." He wished to help?

"I have to wait until Mrs. Hoggard leaves the street," he said with a shrug. "I might as well make myself useful."

Isabella cleared room beside her at the table, a delicious little tickle within trying to make her grin. Of course Miss Thresher was wrong. Isabella knew very few rakes who would deign to help in the kitchen.

"My uncle's apron is hanging in the corner, just there," she said, sprinkling flour over the table for him. She retrieved another rolling pin as Mr. Backus held up the apron as though trying to make sense of it. With a laugh, she brushed her hands on her own apron. "This buttons to your waistcoat." She grabbed the corner with the button hole, and before she realized her actions, looped it over the top button that rested against his chest.

Isabella snatched her hand away. She'd hardly touched him, and yet a strange shock pulsed up her arms as she grazed the silk of his waistcoat with her fingertips. "The ties go around and knot in front," she mumbled, hurriedly turning back to the table.

She busied herself piling a mound of dough onto his work surface. "Roll the pin like this, with the palms of your hands," she instructed before he'd even taken his place. Her own rolling pin flew over her section of dough, flattening it in moments. She set the pin to the side. "Now we will cut the biscuits."

"Wait a minute." He awkwardly turned his rolling pin over the dough. In no time it stuck and curled around the wooden cylinder.

Isabella stopped him and disentangled the rolling pin. "Use more flour. And this time take longer strokes." She dusted the dough and the pin once more. Mr. Backus rolled it in longer movements, but left long dents along the top.

"You nearly have it." Isabella slid an arm between his and placed her hand in the center of the rolling pin for the next roll. "Firm and even pressure."

Mr. Backus paused to regard her. The breath caught in her chest as she lost herself in his brown eyes. The little tickle inside swelled, buzzing through her at a dizzying pace.

"Your parents are doing themselves a great disservice by not paying you notice," he said. "Not many young ladies would care to help a relative in this way."

"Yes, my parents will regret it when I end up a spinster," she said playfully.

He shook his head. "You do them a great credit, even though they do not see it. A better credit than they deserve."

"I doubt that." This was flattery, was it not? Simple teasing, as always. And yet he did not laugh.

He tipped his head forward until their brows nearly touched. Her eyes fell to the top button of his waistcoat peeking through the buttonhole on her uncle's apron. The bright green silk made a stark contrast to the linen's rough fibers.

"I hope you know that you are valued," he said, "no matter what their lack of attention seems to say. Your true friends can see it. Someday the rest of your family will as well."

"And…do you count yourself among my true friends?" She should not have asked, but the words tripped off her tongue.

"I would like to."

Isabella ducked her head, biting her lip. It was as though the oven fires had kindled within her, popping and swelling with a fresh log. A true friend. Perhaps more?

"We should continue," she said with a shaky voice. "My aunt will return soon." She let him finish rolling out the dough, though stepping away from his warmth made her miss the proximity. Focusing on her own batch to try to calm the whirlwind in her chest, she plucked up one of the biscuit cutters in the shape of a little man. Aunt Keppel cut most of the gingerbread into long, fluted rectangles perfect for dipping in tea, but Isabella preferred the silly shapes her aunt made for special occasions.

Mr. Backus took one of the other cutters, a little man like hers, and haphazardly pressed it all over his sheet of dough.

"The best practice is to get the shapes as close together as possible," she instructed, showing him her even pattern.

"Oh. Why is that?"

Isabella carefully lifted her shaped biscuits onto a tin sheet. "The more the dough is worked, the tougher it becomes. Instead of a fine snap when bitten, it becomes hard to chew."

Mr. Backus nodded obediently. "I will try harder to squeeze them as tightly together as two people squished in a sledge." The corners of his lips twitched, and hers threatened to do the same.

He threw his biscuits onto the sheet, leaving the little men lopsided and coated in too much flour. Isabella lifted the filled sheet to examine them. No one would confuse his for hers.

"Those poor little men," Isabella lamented.

Mr. Backus stepped closer. "Come, now. They're only dancing."

"A strange dance, if that's what it is." Isabella blew off the excess flour that covered the disfigured biscuits.

Mr. Backus staggered back, coughing and sputtering with a flour-speckled face.

Her hand flew to her mouth. "Oh, I am terribly sorry!" She quickly set down the baking sheet and searched for a cloth.

He swiped a pinch of flour off the table and flicked it at her face. Isabella gasped at the white cloud, too late throwing her arms up to protect herself. Mr. Backus chuckled and made for more flour.

She dove for his hand. "No! You mustn't." She pinned his hand against the table, but he reached around with his other and snatched some more to dust over her like snow, getting as much on himself as on her. "Some gentleman you are." Isabella released him and swatted at her hair. "My aunt will return any moment."

He went for more flour, but she moved in front of him to block his arm, grabbed a handful, and flung it towards him. A line of flour stretched across his chest, some of it outside the protection of his apron. Mr. Backus shuffled back, laughing.

"Very well, very well. You win. I concede."

Isabella fingered the little mound of flour left on the table. "Swear it. I don't believe you," she said through a breathless giggle.

He swept what he could of the flour from his clothes, then bowed deeply. "I swear not to renew any battle with the lovely Miss Todd, who has won our engagement soundly." Then he caught up her hand and laid a wisp of a kiss across her bare knuckles.

She made to speak, but no words came. The white cloud around them hung suspended in the warm kitchen air, catching light from the window. She should scold him. She should laugh. She should do anything but stand still and gawk.

"Heavens! What happened?"

Isabella jumped at her aunt's voice from the doorway. Mr. Backus straightened and gave a very formal bow, made all the more ridiculous by the flour dredging him head to toe.

"You will forgive me, Mrs. Keppel," he said. "I was trying to avoid Mrs. Cowden in the street and thought to help Miss Todd with her task."

Cowden? Had he not said he was avoiding Mrs. Hoggard when he entered?

Aunt Keppel remained rooted to the floor just outside the kitchen. "Did you make anything more than a mess?" No displeasure tainted her voice, but Isabella still dropped her gaze sheepishly.

"I will sweep it up, Aunt."

"Your father would not be pleased to see you working in the kitchen."

No, he would not. Isabella shrugged. "The gingerbread was low."

Aunt Keppel turned to their guest. "Thank you, sir, but I believe I can help Isabella from here. Your efforts are most appreciated."

Mr. Backus quickly removed Uncle Keppel's apron and gathered his jacket and coat, both bestrewn with a generous sheen of white. How they'd managed to get so much flour everywhere, Isabella did not know. But as he scampered out the door with one last grin and a wink in her direction, she could not be very sorry at the turn of events.

That night, Isabella sat in her room wrapped in a blanket and cradling a cup of tea in her lap. A plate of the biscuits Mr. Backus had made stood on the bedside table nearby. Aunt Keppel hadn't allowed them anywhere near the front counter in their flailing forms.

Isabella picked one from the plate and nibbled off its foot. Mr. Backus had been so kind that day. And not in his usual, honeyed way. He hadn't balked at the sight of her working in the kitchen. She knew very few gentlemen who would have joined her at the table like that.

She snapped the gingerbread man in half, the homey flavors barely registering. When she arrived at Market Foxley, she hadn't considered the possibility of finding a match. Always she believed her parents would do the finding for her, whenever they felt inclined to do the job. Now, it seemed, she had done the job for them.

A wintry wedding in London played out in her mind. Mr. Backus beaming that alluring smile of his as he escorted her from the church with Mama and Papa on their heels singing his praises. Her sisters' masked jealousy at how handsome a husband Isabella had found, her brothers' jokes at her finally catching someone crazy enough to want her. The balls and dinners where she would sit as guest of honor, at last able to display her worth to Society.

I hope you know that you are valued, no matter what their lack of attention seems to say. Your true friends can see it. His words kneaded deep-set aches in her heart that she'd nearly given up on. They'd already begun, to the tiniest degree, to fade, like the soreness in her shoulders after Tuesday's races.

She turned the deformed head of the biscuit over in her hand before tossing it into her mouth. No, this was not how she'd expected her visit to the Keppels' to play out at all. What a beautiful Christmas surprise.

But the best part of standing so close to the laurels of victory—she never dreamed love would taste this sweet.

Chapter Eight

*A*ndrew absently opened his brother's door for his usual morning visit carrying a dish of tea and biscuits sent over from Hinwick's. Something had been nudging at the back of his mind the last few days since helping Miss Todd in the kitchen. Perhaps just the realization that his heart was three-quarters gone to that young lady, but the incessant prodding felt like more.

"Good morning," Steven said from a chair by the window. His servant had parted the curtains slightly, and after so many morning visits in the dark, the sliver of light seemed a brilliant glow.

"How are you this morning?" Andrew handed his brother the cup and took the opposite seat. Steven had more color to him, or was it simply the light?

His brother chuckled as he surveyed the biscuits on his plate. "Gingerbread?"

"Yes, it can help with pain and restore the appetite," Andrew said quickly. "This is the highest quality I could find in Market Foxley."

Steven raised an eyebrow. "I have not even seen Miss Todd since last year, and yet here she is everywhere I turn."

Andrew's ears grew hot. "Miss-Miss Todd? These are from—"

"Her uncle's bakery. Our aunt has spoken of little else to me in weeks."

Andrew avoided Steven's penetrating gaze. That woman would drive him to an early grave. Then he wouldn't have to worry about the whole inheritance business.

"She fears you have been lost completely to 'the little Todd girl.'" Steven took a sip of tea.

Andrew rubbed his brow. He wasn't completely lost yet. Was he? The nagging tap at the back of his mind intensified.

His brother picked up one of the biscuits and examined it, then gave it a tentative taste. "I see nothing wrong with the match. I do not know why the thought irks her so."

"Perhaps because she did not arrange it," Andrew grumbled.

Steven's eyes widened. "Is it a match, then?"

Andrew gulped. A match. He dug the heels of his hands into his eyes. Was it a match? He liked Miss Todd. He liked the way her eyes sparkled when she laughed, and how her family bonds were more important to her than Society's expectations. She didn't beg for praise, even if she deserved it. And most important of all, she hadn't tried to catch him. He didn't think she cared at all whether his uncle gave him the inheritance as expected. He could be simply Andrew Backus in her company, not a London dandy or a country heir.

Was his heart, indeed, all the way gone?

"Admit it," Steven goaded. "You adore her."

"And let Aunt Backus win?" Andrew couldn't hide a grin. "She would find far too much satisfaction in an engagement, even if the lady was not her first choice."

Steven leaned back in his chair. "What are you to do, then? Carry this around forever until another gentleman snaps her up? You complained after Mr. Nicholas's attention to her during the races. You were mad with jealousy."

"'Mad' is too strong a word," Andrew said.

Steven pursed his lips.

"Oh, come, I was not so bad as that."

"Are you frightened to return to London a married man, Andrew?" Steven set his empty cup and plate on a side table and stretched out his long legs. "I never took you for a coward."

Andrew held up his hands. "Marriage should not be jumped into lightly." And he'd never expected to be the first of his friends married. At four and twenty, none of his London comrades had made the step as yet. Some, such as Nicholas and Jacobs, hadn't left university.

He loved the cards and parties and flair of bachelor life in Town. And yet... Could he return to them now without regretting Miss Todd's absence? Every day he spent away from her left him anxious and absent minded. She was a piece of his life he hadn't known he lacked. A piece that brightened his world in a way he hadn't expected.

Could he do it? Could he ask for her hand?

"Shall we make a bargain?" Andrew asked, lacing his fingers around his knee. A curious hitch in his breath set his chest pounding as though he'd run from town.

"What is your bargain?"

Andrew leaned forward, steepling his hands. "If you will attend Aunt's Christmas Eve dinner, I will make an announcement." That would give him just enough time to apply to her father for his blessing, should the roads stay clear for the mail to get through.

A smile slowly spread across his brother's face. "That is a bargain I can try to fulfill." He held out his hand, and Andrew gripped it firmly. Twenty years they'd grown up together on their aunt and uncle's estate. Sometimes it felt as though they had no one but each other, and lately Andrew had wondered if they even had each other anymore. But the joy in Steven's eyes told him that still remained.

This was not to be the Christmas he'd expected when he agreed to his aunt's request of returning to Shropshire for the winter. It was to be far, far better.

Isabella sat in the Cowdens' parlor with Miss Thresher, Miss Bentley, the two Miss Cowdens, and Miss Hoggard. Miss Thresher had insisted they all embroider handkerchiefs for servants for Christmas, though why she had thought to invite Isabella to the event, Isabella could not say. Most of Market Foxley, beyond Mr. Backus, excluded her from social gatherings.

She pulled her needle through to the wrong side of the cloth, making a pretty knot for one of the holly berries on her design. Though she wouldn't see any of her servants until her parents sent for her, she thought Mrs. Martin, the lady's maid who served her and her mother, would appreciate the token.

The eyes of every young lady in the room kept darting back to her. Isabella paid them as little mind as she could. They did not know her well, and naturally they must have curiosities. But stiff silence had reigned most of the morning, rather than conversation, as though they did not wish to know her better.

The elder Miss Cowden asked if anyone desired more tea and set aside her work to prepare it when Miss Thresher answered in the affirmative.

Miss Bentley leaned in to examine Isabella's stitches. "What a lovely pattern, Miss Todd. To whom will you give it?"

That she had secured Mr. Backus's attentions over Miss Bentley, Isabella could not understand. Miss Bentley was a lovely girl, and only her overbearing parents had dissuaded Mr. Backus from showing an interest. A fact Isabella could not lament, in truth.

"I'm sure she plans to give it to her aunt," Miss Thresher said, accepting the cup of tea from Miss Cowden. "Her aunt fits into the category as well as anyone."

Isabella glued her eyes to her work. No need to respond. Miss Thresher wanted an argument, and she would not give it.

"Her uncle, of course, might still be considered a gentleman by some." Miss Thresher sniffed. "Though I cannot imagine sinking so low as that. And he did it of his own choice!" She shook her head, sausage-like curls sweeping across her brow. "His family was right to cut him off for such impertinence."

Isabella bit the inside of her cheek. If she spoke, she would regret it. And yet her heart screamed to defend her dear relations against the abuse.

"But it was a love match, was it not?" Miss Hoggard said in a tiny voice. Isabella shot her a smile. At least they had one romantic in the gathering.

Miss Thresher waved her embroidery dismissively. "One may find a love match in their proper circle. Those who marry beneath them for the sake of love are inexcusable fools. No doubt Mr. Keppel grieves his lost position in Society and rues the day he agreed to such dishonor."

"My uncle has no regrets," Isabella said, fighting to keep the hiss from her tone.

"Then he is more of a dunce than I thought."

Isabella drew in a slow breath. *Keep working.* The others would see the rudeness of Miss Thresher's words.

"And he did not even get children out of the bargain," Miss Thresher continued, as though they were gossiping about some distant acquaintance's family, rather than the family of someone in the room.

"My aunt and uncle are very happy," Isabella said.

"Ah, yes, because they have other forgotten relatives come visit, such as you."

Isabella flinched as the words cut into her. She stuck her needle into the linen and pretended to untangle her thread. She had stayed for nearly an hour. A few more minutes, and she would make excuses to leave.

"Your parents are in London, are they not?" Miss Thresher asked. "Why did you not go with them?"

"Market Foxley is a lovely place to visit at Christmas," the older Miss Cowden volunteered. "It is nice to retire to a quiet village before braving the crowds of London in the new year."

"Have you even had a Season, Miss Todd?" Miss Thresher asked before her friend had finished speaking.

Isabella straightened. "I have not." Time to make excuses.

"Your parents doubt your abilities. No wonder. You cannot seem to catch anyone, not even Mr. Backus."

So that was the reason for this mistreatment. Isabella closed her eyes. Like one of Uncle's steaming ovens with the door firmly closed, her insides seethed, ready to scream out all the horrifying things she could think of to say about the Threshers. She would keep them in. Only a petty child would react.

"I have had much more success, though I do not wish to boast." Miss Thresher brought her pitiful attempt at embroidery closer to her face, as though suddenly engrossed.

"Success?" the younger Miss Cowden asked. The other ladies glanced at each other in confusion.

Isabella swallowed a snorting laugh. Of course Miss Thresher had not found success. It was a lie, clear as the sunny December morning outside the parlor window. How she wanted to toss the contents of the teapot at the young woman and wash the prim smile from her face.

"But you will have to wait until Christmas Eve to learn of it. I have sworn not to breathe a word of it before then."

"We are all used to dining at the Backuses' on Christmas Eve," Miss Hoggard said. "Is that not a strange place to announce an engagement, when at another's party?"

"When at another's party, yes." Miss Thresher scanned the room to make sure she'd caught their attention.

You cannot be serious, Isabella groaned within.

"But when at one's own party…"

Eyes widened around the room as the implication of her words set in. Isabella shook her head. This girl had failed all other attempts at snatching up Mr. Backus, and now she felt the need to stoop so low as to start rumors?

"You are engaged to Mr. Andrew Backus?" Miss Hoggard whispered.

Miss Thresher coyly put a finger to her lips. "It must not be known until Christmas."

She should let it go. Let Miss Thresher make a fool of herself. But the words came spilling out, and Isabella could not stop them. "That is the worst sort of lie I have ever heard. You?

Catch Mr. Backus? That is impossible."

Miss Thresher's cheeks flamed quicker than paper thrown on a fire. "You would not know if he has made me an offer."

Isabella set her embroidery down and tilted her head. "I know you have no understanding, as I have already caught him."

Gasps sounded across the room. A brazenly forward statement. And yet her heart could not keep silent. The warmth in his eyes as he spoke from his soul, the way his gaze lingered on her lips, the feeling of belonging he brought with him every time he stepped through the bakery door—all of it belied his intentions.

"If you have caught him," Miss Thresher said through gritted teeth, "he does not realize it."

Isabella rose and gathered her things. "On the contrary, Mr. Backus does know it. He much appreciated my tactics to your own. And we will announce *our* engagement at the Christmas dinner. Count on it."

Miss Thresher flew to her feet and advanced on Isabella, stopping with their faces inches away. "I do not believe it for one moment."

"Just as I never believed you." Isabella held her ground, but an itch ran along her spine that made her want to shudder. Why had she given in?

"We shall see who Mr. Backus delivers his invitation to first," the young woman said with a sneer. "Of course he will deliver it to his real lover. And I will bring my invitation to you as soon as I receive it."

"And when you receive yours from the Birchill footman, I will already be waiting with mine," Isabella said, stepping away and curtsying to the others, "along with the gentleman in question, who will be taking tea with me in my aunt and uncle's tea room as he loves to do." She thanked the Cowdens for their hospitality and left a sputtering Miss Thresher to be consoled by her friends.

But as she walked back to the bakery the chill only grew,

and not from the winter air. What if she had been terribly wrong about Mr. Backus? She'd laid bare her intentions, and doing so before Miss Thresher was as good as doing so before the world. She gripped her reticule tight against her stomach, which threatened to heave.

He loved her, all his interactions insisted on it, and yet she could not push away the paralyzing thought that she might have ruined everything.

Chapter Nine

This was a good morning for drinking tea.

Andrew walked briskly down the lane leading from Birchill Manor, and though the wind whistled through the trees on either side of him, he took no notice. After all, he had an invitation to deliver. Red-chested robins chortled from branches that dripped melting snow. Though far from a spring day, the morning reflected the lightness in his belly that carried him faster and faster into Market Foxley.

And the only thing to make it better? Tea and gingerbread from a quaint bakery, and the company of a certain red-haired lady with a ready grin.

Andrew always expected to freeze at this step in his life, but today already proved different from those assumptions. His feet could not carry him to Hinwick's fast enough. Miss Todd did not need a fancy speech. A greeting, a joke, a short and sincere declaration, and he would be an engaged man, free from the pursuit of his neighbors.

When he reached the town, he bid Mr. and Mrs. Bentley a good day, but did not stop to let the lady talk. They watched him with curious looks. Did he seem overeager? Undoubtedly.

Another figure approached him, and for once he did not avoid her. He tipped his hat. "Good day to you, Miss Thresher."

He meant to rush past as he had with the Bentleys, but Miss Thresher lashed out and caught his arm with both her hands.

"Oh, Mr. Backus, how good it is to see you."

"Yes, a pleasure." Andrew tried to pull his arm away, but his coat sleeve remained hostage in the young lady's grasp. "If you will excuse me."

"I am beside myself with anticipation of your aunt and

uncle's dinner next week," she crooned. "It is always my favorite tradition."

"A very agreeable party, to be sure." He tugged. His sleeve wouldn't budge.

Miss Thresher stepped closer, going up on her toes. He had to veer backward to keep her from pressing her face against his, like her mother's face had pressed against the window on his first meeting with Miss Todd at the bakery all those weeks ago.

"I anxiously await my invitation, sir." She gasped, bringing one hand to her mouth. "But perhaps you are on your way to deliver one now?"

Not to her. He took the opportunity to pull his sleeve from her remaining hand and retreated a safe distance to give her a bow. "I am certain the invitation will be delivered directly. My aunt prides herself on a prompt delivery one week before Christmas."

"I would much rather it come from a more amiable messenger than the footman." She twirled a curl around her finger.

Dash it all, people across the street were beginning to stare at her blatant flirtation. Including Mr. and Mrs. Bentley, the latter with a scowl.

Andrew stepped back again. "Good day to you, Miss Thresher," he said, a bit louder than politeness called for. Before she could trap him again, he turned on his heel and hurried away.

"Mr. Backus, wait!"

He cringed as the wail echoed down the street. But she did not follow. Thank heavens.

Hinwick's, with its pale green sign and polished windows, appeared around the corner. All tension that had mounted in his shoulders on his encounter with Miss Thresher waned. He pulled open the door to the tinkling of the bell, and there she sat as though waiting. Steam rolled off her cup of tea in a delicate veil across her face while she sipped.

He waited to greet her until she'd lowered the cup, shoving

his gloves in his pocket. Sounds filtered in from the kitchen, but her aunt did not stand at the counter as usual. Relative privacy. It was all he could hope for.

"How are you, my dear Miss Todd?"

She tilted her head, one corner of her mouth twitching. Was he too formal? Had she guessed?

"First, I must give you this." He reached into his coat and drew out the invitation his aunt had written. "I hope to enjoy the pleasure of your company Christmas Eve."

"Thank you," she said, standing and gently taking the folded paper. "I will be delighted to attend."

She gazed up at him, a question in her eyes, and only then did Andrew pause. He swallowed.

This moment, his world changed forever.

Why did Miss Thresher always appear at the worst moments? Isabella caught sight of her across the street as she took the invitation from Mr. Backus. The paper trembled in his hands.

His neckcloth bobbed, and he smoothed the front of his waistcoat. She had never seen him fidget like this. Either he had fallen ill, or… She clasped her hands in front of her. Dare she hope? She prayed Miss Thresher would not interrupt.

"Miss Todd, there is something I wish to say to you."

It took all her concentration not to shuffle her feet. She'd waited for this moment since November. Imagined a gallant proposal and calmly elegant acceptance at least a hundred times. But either the potential of Miss Thresher watching through the window put her on edge, or she failed to comprehend in all those dreams how deeply she would desire these words about to fall from his lips.

"I did not return with the hope of finding a wife." He laughed. "You know as well as I how I've tried to avoid it these two months."

Last night she'd despaired at the predicament her quarrel with Miss Thresher had caused. Now it would be of no concern.

Mr. Backus reached out his hand, hesitated, then took hers in his, pulling her fingers out of the knot she'd tied them in. She shivered at his touch, and not because of his cool skin.

He brought her hand to his mouth and kissed it. "And somehow, despite all my efforts, I've found myself unwittingly, but not unhappily…" Once again he pressed his lips to her hand. His warm breath sent a tingling up her arm.

Never mind her family's notice. Never mind the place in Society. Andrew Backus did love her. Her eyes welled, and the sun shining through the window turned to misty gold. Could the world have shown her a more perfect day, after all her years getting swept into the corner to make room for the rest of her family?

The bakery door crashed open, its bell clanging roughly before falling limp in the holder. Miss Thresher sauntered in, a smug smile on her face.

Isabella tried to pull her hand back, but he kept a tight hold of it. "I did not expect to see you again so soon," he said.

Miss Thresher spoke over him. "Congratulations, Miss Todd. You were victorious, as you claimed."

"Victorious?" Mr. Backus asked.

Isabella shrank back. Why would Miss Thresher do this now? Isabella stood on the brink of everything she'd ever prayed for. This woman wanted to send it all toppling into oblivion.

Miss Thresher tapped her chin. "How did you phrase it? 'I know you have no understanding, as I have already caught him.'"

She wilted under the young lady's sneer, and further when Mr. Backus turned his gaze on her.

"Who said that?"

"Miss Todd, just yesterday." Miss Thresher folded her arms. "We were drinking tea at the Cowdens'."

Isabella's fingers slipped out of his and plummeted to her

side, limp.

"'He much appreciated my tactics to your own. And we will announce *our* engagement at the Christmas dinner. Count on it.'" Miss Thresher spoke in a mocking falsetto.

"You were convincing the others you had an engagement with him," Isabella cried. Her voice came out pinched. "What do you have to say for your own lie?"

Miss Thresher stuck out her chin. "To quote Lyly, 'All is fair in love and war.'"

Mr. Backus's face blanched. He inched backward towards the still-open door. "This was a game to you."

"No." The word stuck in her throat. Of course it had been a game, as much as it had been a game for any of the other families in town. "For several weeks, I have not seen it that way." But hadn't she? Just yesterday she boasted to every young woman in the neighborhood that she had won, dangling it before their noses like a toy. Her knees threatened to buckle so she could curl up on the ground like the forgotten child she still was. It could do nothing to harm her dignity further.

"You were one of them all along," he choked out. "I thought you were different."

A hot tear dribbled down the side of her face. "My feelings are true. I swear it."

He'd nearly reached the doorway, the heels of his boots pounding dully across the wooden floor. "You tricked me."

The accusation rattled her breath. She could not deny any of the charges he laid at her feet. Yes, she had tricked him. On purpose. And while Miss Thresher would gloat about being the cause of this disaster, Isabella could only hold herself responsible.

Before he completed his flight from the bakery, Isabella ran for the stairs, leaving the coveted invitation on the table. Miss Thresher called a sickly sweet farewell. Isabella's footsteps thundered in her ears, hammered in her temples. In the same instant, all her yearnings had been offered and snatched away.

She dove onto her bed and pulled her knees up to her chest. With a sob, she buried her face into the snow-white fabric of her morning dress, the very one she'd worn the first day Mr. Backus stumbled into the shop. Her heart twisted until she was certain the already battered fibers would wrench apart.

Worse than any of it—Mr. Backus's hollow, accusing expression as he backed out of the bakery and her life. No matter how hard she blinked, the vision would not leave her throbbing mind.

Chapter Ten

*I*sabella folded her last gown and set it atop the others in her trunk. One travel dress and her pelisse draped over the chair for tomorrow, but the rest were properly stowed.

A knock sounded on the door. "You may come in," she said, closing the trunk lid. Her small gathering of necessities for that evening and the morning sat on the bedside table. She would throw them in quickly before the coach arrived.

"What did your mother have to say?" Aunt Keppel asked in her soft manner. She must have seen the open letter on the table. "Besides informing you the carriage would come?"

Her mother's letter could not have arrived at a better time. Isabella had just sat down to write Mrs. Backus to inform her she could not accept the invitation to tomorrow's Christmas Eve dinner. Not after last week's confrontation with the woman's nephew and Miss Thresher. Now Isabella had a valid excuse.

"I will be traveling to London with our friend, Mrs. Garrick, and her family. Mama is anxious to acquaint me with a family they recently met." She went to the table and fussed with her belongings, though they didn't need rearranging.

"A family of wealth or title?"

"Title, mostly," Isabella said quietly. "He is a baron." And so far above Aunt Keppel's station.

"With an unmarried son?"

Isabella nodded. If Mama's plans went through, would Isabella ever be allowed to return to the Keppels' snug bakery and tea room? It wasn't a place for a potential baroness, even if the last single son were third in line for the title and unlikely to hold the honor.

Two months ago she would have exulted in this letter. Her parents finally thought to help her secure a comfortable future, one with far more distinction than her sisters' situations. True, they were simply using her to gain social ground, and she was their last single daughter, but it should console her. Heaven only knew which Backus son would end up with the inheritance. In Society's eyes, the interruption of Andrew Backus's proposal had been most fortunate. And if nothing came of the baron's son, at least she would finally get a Season and a chance to improve her situation.

What did fortune or position matter in the end? Aunt Keppel stood before her in faded apron and worn dress. She had no wealth or distinction. Her husband's family had scorned her. Heaven had withheld the blessing of children. But she had a safe home, a comfortable occupation, and an adoring husband. If she had the opportunity to join the tussling gentry, would Aunt Keppel do it?

"I am sorry you will not be spending Christmas with us." Her aunt crossed the room and sat on the corner of Isabella's bed. "We will miss you when we take gingerbread around to our friends and neighbors."

Isabella attempted a smile. "I wish I could stay."

"You loved that young man. It's difficult when things fall apart as they did."

Isabella's eyes stung. She pressed her hands to her face, wishing the tears away.

Aunt Keppel held out her arms. Isabella sank onto the bed and fell into her aunt's embrace until the shaking and sniffling receded, leaving her empty once again save for a tiny spark. Mr. Backus may not have cared any more for her, her parents may not have worried about her happiness, but here above Hinwick's Bakery and Tea Shop, she would always find love.

Andrew stood at attention as his aunt charged down the front hall, a footman trailing after her. She tore off her bonnet, coat, and muff, dropping them unceremoniously. The poor lad tried to catch them before they hit the floor.

"It's all over town." Aunt Backus threw up her hands. "That little fraud told everyone you'd made her an offer. Now it's as good as settled. Thank heavens it will reflect poorer on her than on you." She pinched the bridge of her nose.

No doubt Miss Thresher had aided the spread of the rumor. Andrew stared at his boots. A moment longer alone in the shop, and the rumors would have been true.

"What a way to begin Christmas." His aunt paced in front of him. "It will be on everyone's mind the whole of tomorrow's dinner." She paused and wagged a finger in his face. "But you must act as though nothing has happened. You will pay Miss Thresher, Miss Bentley, the Miss Cowdens, and Miss Hoggard as much attention as ever."

Which was hardly any.

"If we do not give support to the gossip, it will fade quickly." Aunt Backus returned to pacing. "I should have expected nothing less than this from Mrs. Todd's daughter."

Andrew bristled. Though she had wounded his heart and his pride, that young woman did not deserve this slander. "Miss Todd is no more to blame than any of the young ladies in Market Foxley." Miss Thresher had tried the same tactic, after all, but the knowledge of it hadn't wounded him as learning of Miss Todd's deception had.

"Moralless, conniving swindlers, the whole family. I should have known they would return to haunt me."

Andrew squinted at his aunt. Now what was she prattling on about? "I hardly think her parents had anything to do with this."

Aunt Backus halted and whirled on him. "Oh, I suspect they had a great deal to do with it. That was Mrs. Todd's way, even when she was still Miss Keppel."

"You knew Mrs. Todd?" Andrew scowled. "I thought we met them for the first time in Cheltenham two years ago."

"Yes, I've known them for an age. I was..." Aunt Backus heightened her posture. "I was engaged to be married to Mr. Todd."

Andrew's mouth fell open. "You?"

His aunt avoided his gaze. "Yes. And he came to me one evening, begging me to call off the engagement. He was in love with Miss Keppel, but he did not wish to ruin my reputation by ending the agreement. He left me with little choice. He married the flirt three weeks later." Aunt Backus removed her gloves and handed them to the wary footman. "I ended in a better situation than I anticipated. But the moment that Todd girl set foot in this town, I knew she would be just as much trouble to me as her conspiring mother. Young women of no sense and too much flirtation always are."

"I would prefer you not slight Miss Todd in my presence." Andrew set his jaw. "Especially if you have no intention of slighting the other equally conniving young ladies of this town."

Aunt Backus rested her hands on her hips. "I do not know what feelings you may or may not have had for that young woman, but you are better off without her." She stormed up the stairs, muttering what he could only assume to be more criticisms of the Todds' youngest daughter.

His mind keenly agreed with her assessment that he had suffered no great loss in severing ties with Miss Todd. If only his heart concurred.

Chapter Eleven

When Andrew arrived in the sitting room on Christmas Eve, Aunt Backus stood sentinel at the door. She snatched his arm as he entered and pulled him towards the corner.

"I thought you were going to stay up there all night," she whispered. "Your uncle is too ill, and I did not even speak of it with Steven. What kept you?" Her hand flew to her chest as she panted.

"I'm sorry to have worried you." He only wished to avoid Miss Todd, and all the other ravenous wolves, as long as possible. If only one or two of them had been unable to attend. But Aunt Backus said nothing about any refusals to her invitations, and if Miss Todd had refused, his aunt would have crowed about it.

"Lewis already informed me dinner was ready." Her breathing slowed. "Please, go find someone to escort in. The sooner we are seated, the sooner I will find my ease."

Andrew located Miss Bourne, a wealthy spinster whose comfortable house and grounds bordered Birchill. The safest choice. "Might I see you in to dinner, Miss Bourne?"

"Surely there are other companions who have caught your eye," she said, inclining her head to him.

Andrew bowed. "None with whom I would rather walk in than you, madam."

Despite her unconvinced stare, the woman took his proffered arm. His aunt announced dinner, and he stiffly escorted Miss Bourne in, not sparing a glance at the other guests. Aunt Backus would scold him for such a cold welcome to the others, though it would only be one of many things she scolded him for that night.

Forgetting Miss Todd's betrayal had not gone well. Though his aunt would not mind his paying that lady little attention this evening, he also could not forgive Miss Thresher's part in the debacle. He'd leave both young women to the responsibility of other gentlemen.

Andrew led Miss Bourne to her seat and stood behind his chair at the foot of the table. Rightly, it should have been his uncle seated there. If not Uncle Backus, then Steven. A place had been set for his brother, but it remained empty as the guests filed around the table at his aunt's instructions. He sat with the others, studying the gold-tipped plate before him, even though he'd eaten from the same china for twenty years. The hope of Steven attending had pulled him down the stairs. But then, Steven knew of the deception unveiled at the bakery last week. That meant the bargain no longer held.

He did not meet any of the guests' gazes, though each one burned into him as the footmen began dishing out the white soup. Silent questions, unspoken assumptions, and condemning rumors tangled in the too-hot air of the dining room. Andrew pulled at his collar. The holiday prevented him from an early exit tonight. Hours of talking and forced laughter before he could retire to the dark emptiness of his room. And how would he avoid the alluring green eyes that most certainly watched him now? Eyes which he had purposely stopped himself seeking out in the sitting room. His stomach clenched.

"Good heavens, Steven!"

Andrew's head snapped up at his aunt's cry. His older brother, pale but determined, stood at the door in a dark grey jacket. He bowed stiffly, staying in place. His hair, lighter than Andrew's, was modestly styled, and he wore a cravat and waistcoat much too simple for his younger brother's taste. Still, it was the best thing Andrew had seen all evening. He leaped to his feet, his first smile in days splitting his face.

"I apologize for my tardiness, Aunt. And company," Steven said.

Andrew waved him over. "Never mind that. Come sit." He ushered Steven to the foot of the table and took up the empty chair beside Miss Bourne. His rightful place. He could not help the rumors surrounding himself and Miss Todd, but perhaps Steven's appearance tonight would help quell some of the gossip about the blasted inheritance.

"Mr. Andrew Backus, tell us your plans for the new year." Miss Thresher. She sat across the table, soup spoon raised.

"I shall return to London directly after Christmas." He engrossed himself in the thick, smooth soup. She'd done enough. Must she continue to pester him? She began another question, and Andrew turned to Steven. "Do you think this clear weather will hold?"

Steven's eyes twinkled. Speaking to his brother about the weather. Yes, a horrible excuse to interrupt the lady. "I think not. My valet said Sampson in the stables predicted snow tomorrow."

Then they would not have company on Christmas Day. That was a relief.

"What a shame Miss Todd could not make it," Miss Thresher cried, loud enough to quiet the gathering.

Andrew's eyes narrowed. Not here? No red curls poked out through the sea of humanity. The other young ladies looked away as he searched.

Aunt Backus cleared her throat. "No, she has been called away to London and left just this morning to stay with friends in Coventry on her way. She sends her regrets that she could not join us."

Murmurs of polite dismay, and a few barely disguised titters, rippled down the table and dissolved as quickly as they started. Andrew filled his spoon, but did not lift it.

Gone?

He hadn't wanted to see her tonight, but knowing she had left Market Foxley, left Shropshire entirely… His next bite of white soup stuck in his throat. He snatched up his drink before he spewed the soup all over his dinner companions.

"How is your health, Mr. Backus?" Miss Thresher asked Steven. "We've missed you at our gatherings."

"Much improved in the last few weeks."

Miss Thresher followed Steven the rest of the evening, bestowing on him the same devotion she had tried to give Andrew since November. Steven took it calmly, as befit the heir of a fine estate. He didn't run from the attention as his brother had. And though Steven's weakness forced him to retire early, he found it in him to pay respect to each of the unmarried ladies and their families throughout the course of the evening.

Andrew would have helped, but for the gnawing at his chest. Mulled drinks and merry song did nothing to soothe the ache. Each time he lifted his eyes, he looked for her lilac dress among the colorful gowns. He listened for her silvery laugh. Even the spices in the cider drew up memories of toasty kitchens, clouds of flour, and fresh biscuits.

Would he see her in London? He scrunched his eyes shut. Town could not serve as his refuge, but neither would Market Foxley and Birchill. He kept in his corner by the door, blocked from the warmth of the hearth and the chatter of neighbors, until guests trickled from the house.

Aunt Backus went up to bed without scolding him. When a servant came to tend the fire, Andrew finally pulled himself out of his chair and up the stairs.

"That was not as exciting as you promised it would be." Steven's voice broke the silence of the corridor. He stood at the door of his bedroom, a single candle behind him wreathing his form in light.

"I thought it would be more agreeable," Andrew mumbled. His eyelids drooped over paper-dry eyes. Aunt Backus always planned a fine Christmas breakfast before church, but even that would do little to entice him from his bed tomorrow morning.

Steven motioned him into the bedroom, and Andrew

woodenly obeyed. The older brother limped to the window and opened the curtain wide. "Look, it has already begun to snow."

Only a few specks came close enough to catch the candlelight. The rest of the world hid under the mantle of night beyond.

"Perhaps the excitement was missing because of Miss Todd's absence," Steven suggested.

Andrew nodded. Of course that was it. But if his brother wished to talk about his problems in love, Andrew had little to give him tonight. "I should sleep, as should you. Good night, Steven. Happy Christmas."

He turned back towards the door.

"I thought you loved Miss Todd."

Andrew's shoulders fell. He paused before opening the door. "She's just like all the others, Steven. I thought she was different. The only difference was she tried luring me in with friendship before snatching me up."

"Does that matter?"

Andrew blinked. He rounded on his brother, who had sat in one of the chairs. "Of course it matters! How would that not matter?"

"How many relationships begin out of forced interactions?" Steven played with the buttons on his banyan. His voice remained mellow and thoughtful, despite Andrew's shouting. "Did Miss Todd seem happy when she was with you?"

That impish grin as they hid behind the curtains, and again when she urged him to beat Jacobs in the race.

"Did she love you?"

Andrew kneaded his forehead. "I thought perhaps she did." She'd seemed so genuinely pleased to spend time with him.

"Then really all she did was manage the hard work for you."

"The hard work." Andrew snorted. "She thinks, as all the others, that I will be named the heir of this estate." His mouth went dry. "That is..." Did his brother know the rumors?

Steven waved a hand. "I know what they've been saying. I agree with them. Is it not better to have a healthy heir than a sickly one?"

"It is your inheritance. It always has been. I don't want it."

Steven leaned his head to one side. "Even if it would catch you the woman you love?"

"If I cannot make her happy without an estate, do I really want her?" Andrew ran a hand through his hair. Dash it all. Her leaving should have ended this pining and confusion.

"I find it difficult to believe that a woman who helps her poorer aunt and uncle in their bakery cares so much about an estate." Steven planted his chin on his fist and tapped the fingers of his other hand on the arm rest.

A fair point. Blast him. "But how do I know for certain?"

Steven shrugged. "You could ask her."

Andrew gestured towards the window in the direction of the lane. "She's on her way to London now."

"Then you might want to catch her before she gets too far. Who knows how long she'll stay in Coventry?" One corner of Steven's mouth curled upward.

Andrew blew out a long breath. This was why he'd sworn off courtship. How had he let a lady wriggle her way into his heart? She'd captured it soundly before he suspected. If he caught her in Coventry, would she return to the Miss Todd of before, all jokes and charm? Would he find any remorse?

He nodded once, then stalked to the door, fists tightened. His fickle heart sped with each step.

There was only one way to be certain.

Chapter Twelve

*I*sabella slid her fingers down the frosty window pane. Outside a snowy Coventry slept in the grey dawn. The Garricks' manor lay close enough to the city for the rooftops of shops and houses to peek out over the trees.

Servants moved about downstairs preparing for the family's departure, no doubt anxious for the Garricks to be off so they could spend the day with their own families, but even the Garricks' little girls had not yet stirred. It would be a few hours before they left.

Isabella had already dressed in a walking gown and pinned up her hair haphazardly. A hat would cover it most of the day. And with only the Garricks for company, she had no one to please.

She swallowed against the tightness in her throat as she pulled on her coat and gloves. Snow hadn't covered the roads terribly yesterday, which boded well for their journey. A pre-breakfast walk into the town would clear her mind and stretch her limbs ahead of the long carriage ride. She straightened her velvet cap over her hair, just as Mr. Backus had done after their hide in the curtains.

And before she could stop, her mind whirled through the wonderful weeks she spent in Market Foxley. Mr. Backus's teasing, the long talks over tea and biscuits, the scheming to avoid the other young ladies. It had all come to such an abrupt end, leaving her hollow and wishing she'd… What? Not pursued him? She would not have known him so well if she hadn't. Not given in to Miss Thresher's goading? Perhaps. But Mr. Backus deserved to know her original intentions.

Isabella fled from her room and out of the house into the

bright stillness of the wintry day. She walked into town with a servant girl who had already been excused, and when they parted ways Isabella wandered to St. Michael's cathedral where she had attended Christmas services with the Garricks the day before. Few people were about that morning, giving her the solitude she both despised and craved.

The rust-colored spire of the cathedral loomed above her, silent and stern as diminutive snowflakes drifted around it. Isabella kept to the path that encircled the ancient building where the snow only lightly dusted the ground. She folded her arms, squeezing her hands between her arms and sides for added warmth. In her haste, she'd left her muff and stole at the house.

Through the cathedral's colorful panes of glass, a little light moved. She paused to follow its progress through the church, but it stopped only part way up the nave. A clergyman checking the building after yesterday's services? Isabella pressed forward on her walk around the church. She'd soon have to head back or risk delaying their departure. With two days of travel ahead of them, no doubt the Garricks wished to leave promptly after breakfast.

A deep, melancholy tune rumbled from the heart of St. Michael's. The organ pipes beckoned to her heavy soul. She pulled a hand from its warm hiding place to trace it along the side of the building. The haunting notes of the fitting *Coventry Carol* reverberated through the aged stone walls. It wasn't the tingling of Mr. Backus's touch, but the faint vibrations soothed a little of the smarting.

Carriage wheels crunched against the road's frozen pebbles, and Isabella scooted closer to the cathedral's side. It wasn't as though she knew anyone in Coventry with whom she'd be forced to speak, but she did not wish to talk with anyone just the same.

"Dash it all. Stop!"

Isabella spun around. Mr. Andrew Backus tripped out of his still-moving coach as the driver pulled at the reins. He stumbled across the road, without a hat and with greatcoat twisted, until he caught his balance. His tousled brown hair fell awkwardly across his forehead. He brushed it back and straightened his coat. His chest lifted and fell slowly under a crimson waistcoat and matching neckcloth.

She gripped the side of the cathedral, unable to move.

Andrew tramped through banks of snow as he worked his way towards Miss Todd. She stayed fixed to the church's wall like a statue of a saint.

"Why are you here?" Her voice melted into the strains of the organ playing inside the cathedral.

He skidded to a stop before her. Why was he here? A midnight conversation with his brother two days before and the question that would not let him rest.

"I had to know."

She dropped her head, entwining her gloved fingers before her. "You must think very badly of me."

He sighed. There was no denying that.

Her face turned from him, and she trudged farther down the wall. "And I deserve it. All of it."

Andrew had expected at least some denial. He followed, giving her plenty of space. "Then did you become my friend for the sole purpose of catching me?"

"It began that way." He nearly lost her response in the music.

Then he'd guessed correctly. She was no better than Miss Thresher, or any of the others. He halted, the hurt in his chest making it difficult to breathe. What madness. He shouldn't have hauled his moping heart all this way for a confirmation of her deception. "Only began that way?" he asked with a mirthless laugh.

"Yes, but it was not long after that my feelings—"

He held up a hand. "Don't go any further." He backed away. He and the coachman could return to Birchill by nightfall if he hurried. "I was wrong to come." He pivoted, the cape of his greatcoat scratching against the stone wall. Aunt Backus had tried to convince him not to do this. He should have listened.

"I am very sorry, Mr. Backus," she cried after him. "I truly am. I did not wish to hurt you. I did not think someone could actually love me just for being Isabella."

Andrew paused.

"All my accomplishments never turned a single eye in my direction. Not even my parents'."

"It surprises you that someone could?" he asked over his shoulder.

"Could what?"

He should leave. He should run back to Birchill as fast as he could before she snapped him up again. "Love you for being Isabella."

She brought her clasped hands to her mouth, almost as if in prayer. "Did you?"

Run, Andrew.

How could he answer such a question? Though he stood several paces from her now, he glimpsed the tear tumbling down her cheek. He rubbed his dry and stinging eyes. "None of that. I cannot bear it." He fished in his jacket for his handkerchief and crossed the divide to give it to her.

She hesitantly accepted it and dabbed at her eyes, face turning pink.

The least he could do was offer to drive her back to the Garricks' house. The innkeeper's directions suggested it a fair walk from this part of town. It wouldn't delay him too much. Then they could part ways properly. He would return to Market Foxley to finish out his promise to his aunt, and she would go on to London. "Why have your parents called you to Town?"

Miss Todd straightened, attention fixed on something down the street. She cleared her throat. "They wish to... They wish to arrange a marriage with the younger son of a baron."

"Oh." Then he was right to make this quick. He nodded serenely. "Well, that will get you quite a lot of attention." Just what she desired.

"I've tried to convince myself that it will be worth the inconvenience of marriage." Her shoulders slumped. She wouldn't look his direction. "I haven't succeeded yet."

"Is that what marriage is to you? An inconvenience?" Andrew asked.

Her pinched eyes and tightly pressed lips belied her efforts not to cry. She brought the handkerchief to her nose, muffling her response. "Marriage to someone I don't love while leaving my heart behind in Shropshire? Yes, that sounds like a great deal of inconvenience to me."

She was trying to catch him again. Was she not? But she stood hunched, head lowered. His arms itched to take her up and hold her to him, to erase the shadow on her face. Little flakes settled onto her cap and caught in her loose, red curls.

She didn't want to marry the baron's son, though it would please her parents and give her far greater recognition in Society than marriage to Andrew. Even as heir of Birchill, he could not have given her that sort of connection. She still wanted him?

"My brother's health is improving."

Her head came up. "It is? Why, that is wonderful!"

He searched for hesitation, regret, or any indication she would walk away. "It means the rumors should die down about my uncle changing his will. Birchill will go to Steven, as it should."

One corner of her mouth pulled up. "And you are free to continue the thrilling life of a bachelor in London. Just as you wished." A whisper of longing tinted her voice.

Andrew rubbed the back of his neck, stiff from yesterday's drive to Coventry. The tossing and turning last night instead of sleeping surely hadn't helped either. "I have found that life less and less appealing in recent days."

"Perhaps when you return to Town, you will remember how much you enjoyed it."

He sighed, dropping his hand. "No, I don't think I will. I think you've ruined it for me."

Miss Todd cringed. "I am very sorry. And also wish to apologize, while I am begging forgiveness, for what I said to Miss Thresher. I should not have spoken without any agreement between us. When she suggested you and she were to be engaged, the indignation at her lies and jealousy at her implications made my mouth run away from all good sense." She spoke rapidly, green eyes fiery as though Miss Thresher stood before her now with the usual smirk. "I wished to put her in her place for spreading such lies, not thinking for a moment that I was just as guilty as she. I do not deserve your forgiveness, sir, but I—"

Andrew could not help it. He took her face in his hands, and the torrential rant bursting from her trailed off. Her breath released in a slow, hazy cloud.

"I wanted to kiss you that day you fell out of the sledge," he said. Standing here, with her so near, the snow gently falling, and the organ's resonant melody wafting about them, he could not keep his gaze from her soft lips.

She let out an uncertain laugh that faded too quickly. "Shall I fall in the snow?" Her hand swept towards the mounds he had just climbed through. "Would that bring back your desire?"

Andrew chuckled, tilting his head until their brows touched and brushing his nose against hers. Her hands found his, holding them to her face. The stirring in his middle reached a distracting hum, and though the weather tried its best to chill him he might as well have been sitting before a roaring hearth.

She'd used him, yes. Hadn't he also used her at the beginning to get away from the others? All the interactions she had contrived to woo him had led to friendship and laughter. Could he really fault her for the creation of such fond memories?

"I think," he said, "I wouldn't mind so very much if your mouth ran away again. So long as it took mine with it."

That impish smile he could not resist glided over her lips. "I can give my mouth looser rein, if you wish."

His lips grazed over hers before she had finished. He waited, their breath mingling in the frigid air. The first kiss deserved to be savored.

But she'd have none of it.

Her lips hungrily met his as her arms encircled his neck, flattening the silly neckcloth he'd gone out to buy that fateful day he lurched into the bakery. He pulled her snugly against him and earned a breathless giggle as he locked his arms around her. How he'd missed the sense of her closeness and the cadence of her voice. Her lips moved over his, fervent and smooth, and he let her take the initiative. He meant to follow wherever she led.

With a little moan, she drifted away from the kiss and settled her head against his neck. He rested his cheek on her forehead. Snowing or not, he could stand this way for hours with her in his arms.

"Congratulations," he murmured. "You have caught the most chased-after bachelor in Market Foxley." And he did not mind it.

"You'll leave behind quite the trail of broken hearts."

Andrew shrugged. "They still have the real heir of Birchill to squabble over. Mr. Andrew Backus is ready to leave bachelorhood behind, so long as a certain Miss Todd is not opposed to helping him change that status."

She pulled back and raised an eyebrow. "Does marriage scare you so much that you cannot ask directly?"

He tightened his grip and lifted her off her feet until she squealed. With another kiss, just to be certain, he cried, "Will you have me, Isabella?"

She rubbed his nose with hers, gripping his neck as though she had no intention of ever letting go. "So long as you promise that we will spend every Christmas in Market Foxley."

"Eating your aunt and uncle out of their supply of ginger-bread?"

"They might force us to make our own if we did that." She eyed his mouth again, then leaned forward and lightly traced it with her upper lip. A heavenly flutter coursed up his spine.

"I cannot say I would mind that." He slid her back to the ground. "Seeing you covered in flour was the moment I realized you'd snapped up my heart completely." He engaged her lips once more. "Does marriage scare you so much that you cannot give me a direct answer?"

She grinned against his lips. "Yes. Though we must…"

He did not let her finish.

Chapter Thirteen

Silver clinked against china amidst the cheerful hum of wedding guests. Isabella nodded gratefully to well wishes and toasts, sometimes prodding Andrew when he forgot to respond. He'd looped his foot around hers under the table, but his leg sidling up to hers had driven him to more distraction than her, as he'd no doubt intended.

"I do not think I have ever had gingerbread at a wedding breakfast," Mrs. King, her mother's old school friend, said from across the table.

"I find it a welcome addition," Admiral King said from farther down. "If unusual."

At the head of the table, Mama pressed her mouth into a stiff line. She'd protested the oddity, but Isabella had insisted. This was the only wedding breakfast she planned to have. Why not serve the food that had helped bring the event about?

"Avice was sorely disappointed she could not make it to the wedding," Mrs. King went on, in her usual rambling manner. "They are not due in Town until March."

"I look forward to seeing Mr. and Mrs. Spencer Addison when they arrive," Isabella said. "You will like the Addisons, my love."

Andrew's eyes had glazed over once more. This time Steven, who sat on his other side, nudged him.

"Yes. Yes, anything you like, my dear."

Good heavens. They needed to get poor Andrew out of this breakfast. He didn't look like he had slept at all the night before. His brother laughed silently into his napkin, disguising it as a cough.

Isabella couldn't blame Andrew. Though the breakfast on

the sideboard smelled divine, especially the spicy gingerbread, she'd hardly eaten a bite. Perhaps if it had been the Keppels' gingerbread, she'd have tried harder. All she really wanted was a moment alone with her husband.

Her husband. The thought warmed her cheeks like fresh tea poured into a cool porcelain cup.

The weight of his hand sank onto her knee under the tablecloth. *Mercy, Andrew!* At least the cloth covered his actions, though the ridiculous grin on his face gave him away. She forced even breaths until Mama rose from the table to signal the end of the meal.

The Kings and the Garricks bid their final congratulations, while Isabella's siblings filed into the parlor. Andrew walked his brother out to his carriage in London's January sludge. Mama kissed her cheek and hurried into the parlor to coo over her newest grandchild, and once again Isabella was left forgotten.

She surveyed the dining room, which waited for the servants to clear it of food and dishes. For once she did not mind being forgotten. She brought her fingers to her lips as the scene in the church danced through her mind. Andrew standing taller than he'd ever stood, brown eyes twinkling as he made his vow. The sting of her cheeks from smiling too wide. His much-too-daring kiss, which he'd stolen in the coach after the service.

What a beautiful day. And it would only grow in excitement from here.

Isabella raced for the stairs, taking them as fast as her legs would move. She panted by the time she reached her upper-floor bedroom that looked out onto the streets. London had little beauty in the winter months, but she leaned her forehead against the window pane and imagined an exquisite snowy day in Market Foxley. The little park in the square across the street had patches of untainted snow that she could almost conjure into a crisp, white field.

"What sent you running for the hills?"

Isabella beamed over her shoulder as Andrew entered the

room and closed the door. How delicious to silence the warnings of propriety that should have sounded in her head before that morning.

His arms circled her from behind, and he rested his chin on her shoulder. "You looked stunning today," he said. "But then, you look stunning every day." He lifted a red curl that hung down the side of her neck and kissed the ringlet, then the skin it had been hiding.

"Did you know, when I was nine, Mama tried to dye my hair?"

His lips pulled into a frown against her neck. "Why would she do such a thing?"

"My hair was too vibrant for her." Isabella laughed. "I would not hold still, and her maid only managed a few strands before the oak dye was everywhere and all were in tears. I've hardly let anyone touch it since."

He fingered the ringlet once more. Isabella closed her eyes, toes curling involuntarily inside her slippers at the sensation.

"I like it just as it is."

She turned, his fingers trailing along her waist. "A gallant answer."

"And the truth." He cocked his head. "I noticed you only nibbled the gingerbread at breakfast. Did you not quarrel with your mother about them being there in the first place?"

Isabella sighed. "Yes. I'd hoped they'd be as good as Hinwick's gingerbread. Alas, they were inferior biscuits."

Andrew reached into his jacket and slipped out a little brown paper package. Her eyes widened.

"Steven was tasked in delivering this. They are not straight from the oven, but perhaps they will do?" He pulled at the strings and the paper fell back to reveal a handful of biscuits shaped like little men. The rich scent of treacle and ginger filled the room.

Andrew plucked one off the stack and set the rest on her dressing table. He held the gingerbread under her nose until she could not keep a serious face. With a snap, he broke off a piece and carefully put it in her mouth. Her shoulders rose to her ears as she chewed the delightful treat, recalling many happy hours talking in a warm bakery. How thoughtful of her aunt and uncle, and how kind of Steven. Andrew took his own bite, but with as steadily as he watched her chew, could he have tasted any of it?

When his lips sought out hers, she relished the sweet, spicy ginger that lingered across them. She'd set out to catch this man three months ago, not thinking she'd come to cherish him so much as this. And if she never tasted another gingerbread biscuit the rest of her life, or if she never drew the praise and notice of a single other person, she would live the rest of it in as perfect joy as she could ask for with this gentleman at her side.

"Not a bad way to start the year," Andrew suggested when he paused for breath. Her arms slipped around his waist to be sure he kept his rest from the kiss short.

Because she could not have agreed more.

The End

~❖~

Author's Note

Market Foxley is a fictional town based on Market Drayton, a beautiful town in Shropshire, England. Market Drayton is the birthplace of Billington's Gingerbread, which has been making gingerbread with one of the oldest gingerbread recipes in the UK since 1817. I drew inspiration from Billington's for my fictional Hinwick's.

Gingerbread has been around in various forms for centuries and is thought to have been brought to Europe more than a thousand years ago. Gingerbread men can be traced back to the Elizabethan Era, though many other shapes were also used through history.

Coventry is a real city in central England and the origin of the well-known 16th century Christmas song, *Coventry Carol.* While the Garrick family estate is fictional, the cathedral of St. Michael's is a real building. Not much of it remains today after bombing during World War II decimated the church, but its ruins have been preserved and the 20th century Coventry Cathedral now shares the site.

Isabella Todd's hometown of Cheltenham is also a real place, as is Rooke's assembly rooms. For more information on Cheltenham, see my author's notes in All You Wish.

The April 1816 edition of Ackermann's Repository did feature an article about the European royal sledge party, which my characters turned into their own version with sledge races. Based on the extravagance of the real sledges, I don't think very many of the party in Vienna took to racing.

Greensleeves has been around since the 16th century, though it didn't become associated with Christmas until the 1860s when the lyrics to *What Child is This?* were written and put to the tune. There are several interpretations of the original *Greensleeves* lyrics, some giving the lady in question a tarnished reputation and some a chaste one. The most convincing research I found points to the latter, but I leave it to the reader to decide.

I perhaps have given Shropshire a little more snow in this story than usually falls these days. In 1816, England experienced a "year without a summer," resulting in much more snow than usual. This came in the middle of what is known as the Little Ice Age, when the world was in general cooler than it had been in the Medieval period and than it is now, which is why I felt I could use a little more snow in 1817 Shropshire than current weather patterns dictate.

Acknowledgments

A special thank you to my critique group and the ladies of Love Letter Press—Sally Britton, Joanna Barker, Heidi Kimball, and Megan Walker—for allowing me to add to our fairy tale series and helping me with this project. Heidi was a rock star and did all the ebook formatting, for which I am eternally grateful.

And thanks to my critique partner Deborah M. Hathaway for cheering me on, especially during the epilogue and through edits. I'm also so grateful to the wonderful Jennie Goutet, whose critiques were invaluable. I could not have finished this without their support and friendship.

A huge thank you to Alayna Townsend, who took my children for three days straight so I could finish the last chapters of this book. Chapters 8 through 13 would not be here without you.

I'd also like to thank Colette Campbell, Alison Clawson, Stacy Compton, and the above-mentioned Lady Townsend for being my stalwart beta readers. They always catch things no one else does and are a great help in getting my books ready for readers.

A shoutout to Shaela Kay of Blue Water Books for designing this beautiful cover, and to Erica Shifflet for the amazing cover photo. Thank you to Allison Moore for being my perfect Isabella Todd. Their work on this cover brought so much inspiration.

Thank you to my children for playing so nicely together all day long for eight days while I drafted. My family is the greatest support when it comes to chasing this dream.

And most of all, my love and gratitude to my husband, who encouraged his insane, hormonal, morning-sick, and

all-too-determined wife to reach her goals.
Someone give that man a medal.

About Arlem Hawks

Arlem Hawks began making up stories before she could write. Living all over the Western United States and traveling around the world gave her a love of cultures and people, and the stories they have to tell. She graduated from Brigham Young University with a degree in communications and emphasis in print journalism, and now lives in Arizona with her husband and two children.

Follow Arlem Hawks on Instagram, Facebook, and Twitter @arlemhawks, and visit her website at www.arlemhawks. com to sign up for her newsletter.

Made in the USA
Coppell, TX
29 January 2020

15149539R10059